# VOICES IN THE DESERT

## AN ANTHOLOGY OF ARABIC-CANADIAN
## WOMEN WRITERS

PROSE SERIES 63

Canadä

ONTARIO ARTS COUNCIL
CONSEIL DES ARTS DE L'ONTARIO

Guernica Editions Inc. acknowledges support of
The Canada Council for the Arts.
Guernica Editions Inc. acknowledges support from the Ontario Arts Council.
Guernica Editions Inc. acknowledges the financial support of the
Government of Canada through the Book Publishing Industry Development
Program (BPIDP).

# VOICES IN THE DESERT

## AN ANTHOLOGY OF ARABIC-CANADIAN
## WOMEN WRITERS

EDITED BY ELIZABETH DAHAB

**GUERNICA**
TORONTO·BUFFALO·CHICAGO·LANCASTER (U.K.)
2002

Elizabeth Dahab, Guest Editor.
Guernica Editions Inc.
P.O. Box 117, Station P, Toronto (ON), Canada M5S 2S6
2250 Military Road, Tonawanda, N.Y. 14150-6000 U.S.A.

Distributors:
University of Toronto Press Distribution,
5201 Dufferin Street, Toronto, (ON), Canada M3H 5T8
Gazelle Book Services, Falcon House, Queen Square,
Lancaster LA1 1RN U.K.
Independent Publishers Group,
814 N. Franklin Street, Chicago, Il. 60610 U.S.A.

First edition.
Printed in Canada.

Legal Deposit — Third Quarter
National Library of Canada
Library of Congress Catalog Card Number: 2002104958
National Library of Canada Cataloguing in Publication Data
Main entry under title:
Voices in the desert : an anthology of Arabic-Canadian women writers
(Prose series ; 63)
ISBN 1-55071-169-5
1. Canadian literature (English) — Arab-Canadian authors.
2. Canadian literature (English) —Women authors.
I. Dahab, Elizabeth. II. Series.
PS8235.W7V66 2002  C810.8'09287  C2002-900484-5
PR9194.5.W6V66 2002

# TABLE OF CONTENTS

Acknowledgements . . . . . . . . . . . . . . . . . . . . .   6

Introduction by Elizabeth Dahab . . . . . . . . . . . . .   7

Anne-Marie Alonzo, *Lead Blues* . . . . . . . . . . . .   17

Andrée Dahan, *Spring Can Wait* . . . . . . . . . . . . .   31

Abla Farhoud, *Dounia-a-World* . . . . . . . . . . . . . .   46

Yolande Geadah, *Veiled Women, Unveiled Fundamentalism*   68

Nadia Ghalem, *Blue Night* . . . . . . . . . . . . . . . .   88

Mona Latif Ghattas, *The Double Tale of Exile* . . . . . .   99

Nadine Ltaif, *The Metamorphoses of Ishtar* . . . . . . . . 104

Yamina Mouhoub, *The Moment Matters Not* . . . . . . . . 109

Rubba Nadda, *Daughter of Palestine* . . . . . . . . . . . 117

Bio-Bibliographies . . . . . . . . . . . . . . . . . . . . . 130

# ACKNOWLEDGEMENTS

The editor and publisher express their gratitude to the following for allowing them to reproduce their work in this anthology:

Anne-Marie Alonzo and Guernica Editions for the selection from her book of poetry, *Lead Blues* (1990).

Andrée Dahan and Éditions Quinze, for the selection from her novel, *Le Printemps peut attendre* (1985).

Abla Farhoud and L'Hexagone for the selection from her novel, *Le Bonheur a la queue glissante* (1998).

Yolande Geadah and VLB éditeur for the selection from her book, *Femmes voilées, Intégrismes démasqués* (1996).

Nadia Ghalem (sole holder of rights) for the short story selected from her collection of short stories, *La Nuit bleue* (1991).

Mona Latif Ghattas and Boréal for the selection from her novel, *Le Double conte de l'exil,* (1990).

Nadine Ltaif and Guernica Editions for the selections from her books of poetry, *Les Métamorphoses d'Ishtar* (1987) and *Entre les fleuves* (1991).

Yamina Mouhoub (sole holder of rights) for the selection from her book of poetry, *Qu'importe le moment* (1999).

Ruba Nadda and Sister Vision Press for the selection from her collection of short stories, *Daughter of Palestine*, in press.

# INTRODUCTION

## Quebecois-Canadian Voices of Arabic Origin

I am grateful to Antonio D'Alfonso of Guernica Editions who welcomed and encouraged this project back in 1996 when I contacted him from Los Angeles for the first time, seeking to elicit his interest. His enthusiasm, his support and his own writings have been a guiding force and an inspiring factor all along.

I had been engaged since 1994 in the archaeological work of finding and identifying, classifying, surveying and accounting for a growing body of literary texts which fall under the rubric "Arabic-Canadian," addressing questions about the writers who produced these texts: Who are they? What is their social and ethnic background? When and perhaps why did they emigrate to Canada? What did they write, how much, in which language and how? With some difficulty and a great deal of persistence, I located and contacted the writers and their publishers; scanned libraries and bookstores for their works; ordered their books; requested submissions, and went to Canada several times to meet with the authors. Little by little a clear picture was emerging against a hazy background: There exists in Canada a literature that was born in the 1970s at the hands of first generation Canadians of Arabic descent. This literature shows the indelible marks of genius and has produced great works in a significant amount. It was produced in all genres and covers styles ranging from the realist to the post-modernist. It is written in French, English and Arabic, thereby fulfilling twice over the definition given by Deleuze and Guattari to minor literatures. It bears the indelible mark of exile, and can presently join ranks with "other solitudes" Canada has come to acknowledge, admit and embrace. Arabic-Quebecois/Canadian literature is differentiated from other minority literatures in that it manifests an internal structure and it is closely linked to the cultural group from which it rose.

With one or two exceptions, Arabic-Canadian writers immigrated to Canada between 1963 and 1974 inclusively. They settled mostly in Quebec and Ontario in this order. The vast majority of those writers are in their forties or early fifties, a relevant fact if one wants to predict the future of this literature. They write plays or documentaries for Radio-Canada or Radio-Québec; they are radio-announcers, film-script writers (Nadia Ghalem), stage-directors (Mona Latif Ghattas) or write for Les Grands Ballets Canadiens (Anne Marie Alonzo). They contribute to newspapers, literary magazines and reviews such as *Le Devoir, La Voix métèque, Trait d'union, La Presse, Liberté, Voix et Images, Humanitas, Canadian Fiction Magazine, The Whig Standard, The Georgian, The Athenian*. At least five of them teach in some capacity at L'Université du Québec à Montréal (UQAM). In Quebec, they are published mostly by non-mainstream publishing houses such as Leméac, L'Hexagone, Éditions des Femmes (Paris), Éditions du Noroît, Hurtubise HMH, Vlb éditeur, Boréal, L'arbre, Guérin littérature, Guernica, Éditions du Noroît, Éditions XYZ, and La Presse.

Some of them are mediators who played a significant role in the transmission and diffusion of their own and other writers' products through the publishing houses and literary reviews they founded.

Especially worth mentioning is York Press founded by Saad Elkhadem in 1974 where he published his entire Canadian production in bilingual (Arabic-English) editions, and *The International Fiction Review* he created in 1975. Another major mediator of this literature was the Egyptian Antoine Naaman who founded and headed Éditions Cosmos in 1969 and Éditions Naaman in 1973, two publishing houses which existed in Sherbrooke up to 1990, four years after Naaman's death. About 10% of Arabic-Canadian literature was published by Naaman.

The thorny part of Arabic, or by extension any minority literature produced in Quebec, is that it is conceived of as being produced by minorities twice removed from the dominant systems, namely the French and English Canadian literary institutions. The first degree of removal would be the political alienation in which Quebec itself, with its own French language, stands in relation to the rest of Canada: a minority within a majority. The second degree of removal for the foreign-born writer would be precisely her foreignness, her hovering at the periphery of major systems whether or not she writes in the language of the two Founding Nations. If she opts for French as a means of integration into Canadian society, she will infuse it with her alienation, for hers is the language of exile, an obnoxious language in search of form, one which rewrites syntax, or has the insolence of doing so. Deleuze and Guattari call it *reterritorialisation* (37). Others call it *écritures migrantes*. So many rubrics under which critics have snugly pigeonholed minority literary voices with the natural consequence of exacerbating their marginality, albeit in so doing canonizing this marginality within the larger new post-modern tradition of a "plurality of centres."

Even though the choice of language by the minority writer has been considered a key issue in the study of multilingual Canadian literature, it bears some artificiality which is worth pointing out. Didn't Heidegger assert that we do not speak a language but that we are bespoken by one? Likewise for a bilingual or a multilingual writer who opts for one language rather than another. In her literary creative activity, she is "chosen" by the language which, for subconscious reasons, at a certain point of time, she feels closest to. Naturally, she can rationalize and provide reasons *aposteriori*, especially if solicited to do so. Those reasons are very interesting to mull over, but the onset of her decision as to the choice of language, I believe to be, as a rule, spontaneous and involuntary.

This is obviously true for Arabic-Canadian writers, some of whom grew up in their country more versed in French as a language of thought and creative expression than in Arabic (as is the case with Alonzo, Ghalem, Karamé, Ltaif, Ghattas, Varoujean), because of the very strong presence of French culture among the upper social classes in the Middle East. Being already francophone, and having emigrated to Quebec, the choice for those writers was a natural one. In the words of Anne-Marie Alonzo: "C'est une langue que j'aime. Mes parents sont venus s'établir au Québec parce qu'on y parlait français. Pour moi la langue française est la plus belle" ("It is a language I love. My parents settled in Quebec because French is spoken there. To me, French is the most beautiful language," Dupré 238). Opted for English are

those writers who emigrated to English Canada at a fairly
young age (Rubba Nada and Marwan Hassan). Those who
left their native country at an older age, such as Kamal
Rostom, continued to write in Arabic, sometimes becoming
writers/translators. Such is the case with Saad Elkhadem who
settled in New Brunswick at the age of thirty-five. In his own
words, Arabic affords him "a direct line without pause or
hesitation between [his] ideas and the images [he] uses"
(telephone conversation with the author in June 1994).
Roughly 15% of Arabic-Canadian literature is produced in
Arabic, while 60% of it is written in French, and 25% in
English.

When I realized soon after I embarked on this worthy project
that I was dealing with more than three dozen authors of
both sexes, the task of having to select works from amidst
that large body of fine writing became somewhat cumber-
some, if not premature. The idea was suggested to me in
1997 by Antonio D'Alfonso to limit the scope of the project
and to devote that first step in the direction of institutional-
izing this literature to the literary production of women of
Arabic background writing in Canada. I found the suggestion
timely and appealing.

The present anthology features nine women writers,
eight of whom live in Quebec, and one in Toronto. Almost
half of them, namely Alonzo, Ghattas, Geadah and Dahan,
come from Egypt; two of them, Ghalem and Mouhoub,
come from Algeria, while Farhoud and Ltaif come from
Lebanon, and Nadda from Syria. They have various religious
backgrounds: Coptic-Orthodox, Catholic and Moslem.
They are often trilingual. The languages mastered amongst
them, other than Arabic, are French, English, German and

Italian. Many have multiple ethnic origins, some very distant, others more immediate. The Egyptian-Quebecois
writer Anne-Marie Alonzo, for instance, has Maltese, Pales-
tinian and Syrian distant origins.

The earliest work by an Arabic-Canadian woman origi-
nated from the province of Quebec, fertile ground for Arabic-Canadian writers of both sexes: This was a work by
Anne-Marie Alonzo, recipient of The Order of Canada
(1997). She had made her début in Paris with *Geste* (1979)
and *Veille* (1982), fragments of poetic prose. In 1983 appeared her *Blanc de thé* in Montréal followed by *Droite et de
profil* (1984) followed by her book of poetry, *Bleu de mine,*
which won her the prestigious Prix Émile Nelligan in 1985.
The number of publications flourished in the 1980s and
stabilized in the 1990s with names such as Alonzo, Ghalem,
Ghattas, Ltaif and Farhoud leading the way. New names
materialised, creating the impression of an instant feminine
literature of Arabic descent.

Books of poetry appeared. Nadia Ghalem brought out
*L'Exil* (1980) and Nadine Ltaif published *Les Métamorphoses d'Ishtar* (1987). In 1981, Nadia Ghalem brought out
a collection of short stories, *L'Oiseau de fer*, followed by her
novel *La Villa désir* (1988) which was a finalist for the 1987
Grand Prix Littéraire Guérin. Alonzo came up with *Écoute,
Sultane* (1987). Mona Latif Ghattas brought out in Cairo her
poetic novel, *Nicolas, le fils du Nil* (1985), and in Montréal,
*Les Voix du jour et de la nuit* (1988), followed by her novel,
*Le Double conte de l'exil* (1990). Andrée Dahan published
her first novel, *Le Printemps peut attendre* (1985), Alonzo
came up with *L'Immobile* (1990), exploring themes of pa-
ralysis, movement, separation, and harrowing physical pain,
and Farhoud published Le *Bonheur a la queue glissante*

(1998), a novel which has been nominated for the Prix France/Québec. Yolande Geadah produced *Femmes voilées* (1996), an essay on young Moslem women wearing the *hijab*, which was one of the finalists for the Governor General Award (non-fiction category).

What unites this bilingual body of writing into one literary system are *partially* recurring themes, often in binary oppositions, which permeate it: acculturation, duality, discrimination, unemployment, freedom, alienation between parents and children, memories of wars, the Canadian cold weather, poverty and prosperity. The vision of the country of origin from the vantage point of *exile* is not an uniform one amongst the writers. For those who left at a young age, the memory of their first country is vague, hinging on the mythical. Such is the case with Ghattas whose Set El Kol in *Les Voix du jour et de la nuit* is a transcendental figure of an eternal Egypt. Such is also the case with Alonzo who will assert in her interviews: "C'est une Egypte mythique dont je parle dans mes livres" ("The Egypt I speak of in my books is mythical," Dupré 248).

Arabic-Canadian women writers may have in common some modalities of an "immigrant experience," however, as with other Canadian writers, they are concerned with a great array of issues, personal, interpersonal, social, political, aesthetic, philosophical and artistic. This diversity is important to underscore so as not to draw *a priori* appraisals and conclusions.

One striking feature of this writing is the diversity of the genres it harbors and the styles it embodies, from the realist strain of Farhoud and Nadda to the post-modern experimentations of Alonzo, Ghattas and Ghalem. In fact, as is the case with a segment of this literature, it is the very notion of genres which seems to have undertaken a major reshuffling. This is especially true of Alonzo, who, whenever possible, *intentionally* puts the caption *fiction* or *contes* in the inside cover of her books, which mostly consist of snatches of broken, fragmented, dismantled poetic prose. However, this "seamless collage [is] unified by a narrative tension never far from the surface" (Jakobson 3). A tension which functions as "a ceaseless rediscovery of the themes of Self, Exile and Other" (Jakobson 3). Would this rediscovery preclude the strict division by genres? Aware that her categorisation does not fit the usual definition, she asserts when questioned: "Mais je suis consciente du fait que mes livres n'entrent pas dans la définition des contes et des fictions. Je préférerais ne pas avoir à les définir. Mes écrits sont à l'image de ce que je suis, à l'image de ma vie. Hybrides" ("I am aware that my books do not fit the usual definition of tales and fiction. I would prefer not to have to define them. My writing reflects my life and my being: Hybrids," Dupré 241).

I have limited my selection to writers who have previously been published and primarily to those who have two or more books in print. In this way, the anthology could serve as a sample of their work and readers may be directed to seek out other books by the authors. To facilitate this task, I have included a full bibliography of each of the writers represented in this anthology. This is an English language anthology meant to acquaint anglophone readers outside Quebec with the writing of Canadian women of Arabic origins. Most of the texts were originally written in French and are included here in English translation. All translations are identified, with the name of the translator following the English text. Most of the texts have never been published before in English translation. The genres represented in this anthology are in the forms of essays, poetry, short stories and scenes from novels. I hope the current selection of texts will be enjoyed and appreciated by many readers.

Elizabeth Dahab
Long Beach

## WORKS CITED

Deleuze, Gilles and Felix Guattari. *Kafka: Pour une Littérature Mineure*. Paris: Les Editions de Minuit, 1975.

Dupré, Louise. "Écrire comme vivre: dans l'hybridité. Entretien avec Anne-Marie Alonzo." *Voix et Images* 56.2 (Hiver 1994): 238-249.

Jakobson, Walter. "Breathing Words: Exile in (other); Towards a poetics of Anne-Marie Alonzo," unpublished talk delivered at a conference on "L'écriture des femmes migrantes en France et aux États-Unis," Concordia University (Montréal), June 30, 1994.

# ANNE-MARIE ALONZO

## LEAD BLUES

Closed! my universe.
And the rest with it. The body kept.
(You know)
and I only see elsewhere blood moves.
Like mine.

So little vein
So very barely red.

I auscultate.

Each savage beat of the heart
each pulse galls me

You write me I remain!

I wait for the imminent
to burst forth.

Only then        in the lowest of light
so brief I know that dreaming
and closed
the pledge will be redeemed.

Let the bird escape this time.

I ask you is this the beginning. This hunger.
All the petals

Like roses flowering from autumn to May.
You plant and from the finger rises
I've only a truce
and dip my dead hand.

Cut off what won't happen.
I listen            and the kneeling angel falls silent.

The bark is on in years.

I brush against   head curly hair brown
filaments of snow          and lead.

Mad for colour if you say for love.

I wait for the leaf to fall cover carpet of glass.
You say past life is born of magic and fine rain.

Writing you mirages
and coupled clouds.

A fingerprick sticks up and pain pushes in from
all around. The bruised fold of flesh opens the
bone stretches sticks through
the skin like scales.
But all my fingers force bends each
in shape not stirring or animate
only thus remaining mute.

The weight of by myself rises.

In the fields by the wood joy ripe to the touch

you're swimming          and from afar a distant hint
of murmurs and whispers.
Drowning and naked you make ripples of the rings.
And ecstasy      but in a second the smile slides
off like everything before the absence.

Your hand my cheek.

And all the languages.

You place (yourself) and I sense losing breath
loved I would overcome.

The mouth works for the sculptured scream.

So many respects.

I exult and halt take time caress
I await the arrival and death and once-lived-life
of this once more.

In total silence ill at ease I'll place one foot
in front          and side-by-side with you will lay my
hand upon your waist.

Of all terrors words.

I graft meaning to every passage.

Others talk! disbelieving their eyes but
I'll write and laugh        in them

I type my pages classed and wet
but never with ink.

My lettered mouth and lead blues.
The bloodlines live on love
and trace this simple word upon the tongue.
Just to know      and remember!

I'll write like a rolling stone.

Then in rush the spasms and colours of gloom.
On the melting snow dissolving under the golden
crust mourning. Living glazed I'll hold myself
erect and cast in ice.

From books to the one
sentences peel off.

What's new these years of plenty
and where does the pain incubate
if nothing exchanges.

From you I need help and soul from you I need
age.

Muted then the mood spreads that speaks of love.

The writing sowing somewhere else.

Listen only to the glint of pain
and so deny all that remains of flight.

Of life are woven woes
the days dissolve to live a bit
a lot!    dissolve.

I hesitate you see.

I shout and cry out from silence
(the words deaths wait for me noisily
their pledge).

Writing my only hope.

So the sentences run together under words
and the point arrives alone this point of love.
Let the bird sing out
dune flight.

Blond letter unreceived.

From you        from you springs everything
purple-rose-lilac
and blue-of-purple-rose.

Soft your starry voice your voice of wind
carries me up as if the sky had opened
nebula showers and yawning ursus amber.

You live trussed up somewhere in pain
but live.

Covered in laughter you roll and collapse
and carry your hands high.
Alive and long as you wish
saying within me there is the sense.

No longer afraid of you
of another storm
the body hides
sleeps bent.

You write (me) these days post to post and

little steps.

Reading christens me I read newborn
and seek in concert body words
and body woes.
I learn to read
the dying cut phrases.
Something to read to say
your notes ring out I listen to the step.

Emerald sparkling rubies under nails.

Raise your sailed voice
softly so terrible.

You sing          inside I cup the echo          tied
harmonic voices tracks allied.

On your breath ear exhausted
alone you soar in chorus.

(Veer off *voce* this bell ringing unanswered!)

Your voice a willow of mist eyes brimming with
tears you stroke brush up against me lightly
raising breath and hope.

How beautiful! you are.

And what opera these songs enchant me.

In evenings like silk I rest and cover up
and this (your) voice of sail
all the dreams asleep
and the finest of all.

I said you sing I say you make me melt
mouth and lips.
The way at last time runs down
with no meals between or after.

I no longer eat or digest.

Living on looks I accept and order
menued *à la carte*.

Bring (me)!
Quail and pheasant and *coq sans orange* but
shrimp over all lobster and crabslegs crayfish
fresh oysters cheese and every heart of palm
artichokes beets and pickles of the kind asparagus
and *gratins* frogs and sometimes octupus salads
and mint-leaves fennel *pâtés*.

And tomato.

These dishes like words.

Greedy forger I build fables
and castles in chocolate.

And mostly you invite me to eat go out and eat.

So from you the knowledge of fine liqueurs
never sweet I call for strong drink
rising liquid burning from the core
hotter than woodfire.

And you serve me dishes at work in the kitchen.

I ask little pepper or very little.

Small servings cubes of meat vegetables
a single meal these two days eating beyond me.

You take the time patient not pushing or forcing.

A mouthful or two slide down
a tear of wine.

Sitting back bent and appetite.
Never hungry in the morning forgetting lunch
and at night again but bent fatigue
a glass of water and cheese.

All meat isn't good to

You never insist          with you I swallow and chew
and I savour.

Recipe books I say        create!
drop the words and wonders.
From phrases to book the story takes a fancy.

I'll build.
Poems and scents wrapped to taste
as if shared prepared with you by me.

Beautiful state this grace.

But       too hot or cold useless isn't it
to try since nothing goes down.
Barricaded upstairs in the palace drunk on aromas
and rocking       sleeping names
my tongue and taste buds numb.

Seated (thus) I have my fill.

Spoon raised fork
sealed in lead.
Then    like children      open the gate and the
plane the car growls its brakes (you say) so to eat
swallow and hold.

Always in mourning waiting creped.
Neither fruit of mango nor juice desserts and
winter suppers nor this queenly choice      neither
eating nor climbing these steps on foot.

And the banquet table must be set the crystal
ringing! the stemmed glass        pouring running
squeezing the essence of white this wine.

Surrounded       music I search for the clarinet
and violin reed or bow draw the lament from the
dream.

Only there the toneless body will touch
touched the heart.

Thus coming and going and nothing left but the
licked plate dreaming I say        you know       my lips
offered awaiting the only sustenance a kiss.
All appetite springs from you.
From your tongue to mine and in other ways the
food all settles you drink and me by your mouth.

But alcohol draws me back thrusts me forward
and draws me back again.
From your eyes and lids I hungrily embrace
push away the glass and mist push away the glass.

Let me reach!

From my hand yours rests warm
from my shoulder to my breast.

From you to me this feasts hunger spreads
I eat at last and chew.

I say tell me about the nile emerald and sapphire
of long mingled waters in imagined memory.

Of silver thread and silken thread I'm listening
ancient history all the omens.
That after me gone grown before me lived
you know        colour buoying up the earth.
It's there the fact draws breath.
Sister near unknown heart you are like me
teach me about wind and air
about held breath.

I say     you fall silent    the word of a friend
awaited from the bottom of time            muted
alexandria born the world          born at last and
round all-bathed in history and well before seeing
knew everything.

Everywhere        and around      like white cloud
childhood life.

The same in fact.          Yours.          You also know
that elsewhere was is no more.

Mad cities sands and dunes a grain encrusts
engraves and from the end of nights
updated memory.

Temples all unknown

all halls and pyramids forgotten
I knew never saw the tracks

Brief country dying for me erased.

At home called rooms ribbons of spume
sailboats and cliff          from horizon to.
So        and wait!          from my mother to yours living
telling taste of coffee olives cumin ocean waves
and scarabs on our fingers.

Passageway of snow revolt
the slightest exile thought.

Having only from the country implored.

(In arab the german school I compose cartridges
of blue and powder I shape the core.)

Coming to me from the source fine features
and reflected browns.

You shooting star firstborn already born
unknown and unfamiliar.
your name cast in hope
your name hope sung.

Thunder waves on the rock I see far
I listen
and gather in heavy sand the fault.

This life is nothing anything else chosen breaks
me down.

Predict r.s.v.p. if the idea will come

from counterfeit travels.
Seated waiting            telltale            a thousand and one
these nights will make history.

From that moment must one cry out?

Perhaps whimper and protest      it's you!            alone
accomplice you've got the key I know it.

And the asses came trotting horses mares mixed
afloat the dozing barquesand surging from the
mirage the dream the rising wreck.
Under palms and figtrees greying temples
And I'm slipping slipping away afraid that in the
beachcorner the image lived now blurs.

I say then sister tell me about the nile.

That the slightest word may unravel the threads
the slightest state unstring and create from far
history small history life.

These lines of visual eyes and sight.

How to silence and proclaim
this city born within me.

From ice or cement but disarmed the breath cuts.

From afar peace and soft principles
Closeby loading.

A ball instinct fires.

This red

and blue
and white flower.

Everything here is in play
this hour changes its metal.

Follow and live.

As the country trusts alloys the people and the
space. And the white of exile melts.
Through love alone the land lives.

Look     and if face changes me the years and ages
heaped and classed.
And the more lined the more hollow flesh
glows with fresh blood.

More desert than snowscape.

And the disappearing steps
melt away like the day.

Outside rain whitewashed houses and terraces
weakened for life to move in seize it all
the moment see it all and change touch and try.

For another country to move in.

Changing language        listening.
(I'm from here from life.)
Fake the pulse push on through blurred curves
the foreign cancelled gap.
(Not being from here like before.)

Nothing is alike that's not begun together.

So each time holiday passes without me.
(The accent especially colour and taste
to eat and drink like dressing
so unlike alike.)

To be a part.    Most of all.

Set off          from afar creation.
Choose           find the essence of the country.

*Translated from the French by William Donoghue*

# ANDRÉE DAHAN

## SPRING CAN WAIT

Islet Street is not really a street because it is, in fact, a dead-end. To make matters worse, it is poorly labeled, like all the streets in this *polyvalente*; nevertheless, at first one sees a certain charm in this setting. It is a low street dotted with brightly-colored doors that attract attention like the outrageous make-up of a circus clown. Maya teaches behind these walls where posters displaying huge, incongruous landscapes with eternal springs and jade-colored seas line up like windows.

She returned out of necessity, not by chance or in passing or out of curiosity, to see what an empty classroom is like, but to be aware of the pain, as when one cuts away the swollen flesh surrounding an ingrown toenail. She opens the door, and all the secret wounds written on the shifting sands of the subconscious dream open along with it.

The classroom had emptied, all at once. The students never wait for the end of the lecture. As soon as the bell rings, there is a noisy scramble to the outside world. It is the same every night. It is 6:00 pm. Maya can heave a deep sigh of relief – the exuberance of children is contagious – through mimicry she too can rejoice over the prospect of a long weekend, but she knows that the bell that rings and the door that opens only release her to a minefield. Anguish, heart-rending pain, and bitterness had lain in wait for her for four months. A student had written *School equals nightmare* on the hallway wall.

She came to them unaware, rich with the culture and prestige that enveloped her as a simple dress, a bit out-dated, and in the end non-existent. They criticized her clothing for its gaudy colors, its sumptuous and nearly eccentric shapes, its slightly too perfect cut, and its flimsy fabric. She loved to look at herself, twirl about, and admire the colors; she did not realize, she did not understand that a foreign gaze perceived her differently. Maya still suffered because they saw marks on her skin that did not exist, because they failed to recognize the grace which she thought suffused even the least of her movements. Reality was no longer the same, and she had been shaken by the change. She began to doubt herself – like someone who wonders, because she is not an expert, if the stones in a piece of jewelry might be nothing more than common shiny objects after all – she even began to question her worth. And there she was: Maya, demoralized, as if robbed of a portion of herself, on the verge of entering an abruptly empty classroom, emptied, void of meaning, as if responsible for the alarm that had covered her features since school reopened its doors.

School equals nightmare. She knows very well that this departure by no means gives her access to the celebration. She is going to leave, disillusioned, adrift, like a floating island traveling on a road made from equal parts of the misgivings, hopes, and regrets that make up her immigrant skin.

Had she at least pondered the events? Had someone warned her? But who could have? Certainly there had been a number of immigration offices, but nowhere had it been an issue of culture or of shock and even less of difficulty or of willingness to adapt. She had met nothing but very young officials, handsome bureaucrats, short-sighted and tight-lipped, relying on superiors tied to a distant department; these were the officials who had talked to her about diplomas, certificates to validate, and medical visits. Thus, measured, judged, recorded, frozen, labeled, and pinned, they had placed her in the file cabinets of the ministry.

No longer an emigrant once on Canadian soil, she assumed the official title of a landed immigrant and stepped out of the airport, protectively replacing the fragile, nearly derisive emblems of her culture, education, and experience in her large brown briefcase. She was certain that she would not adopt this country until it adopted her.

What had they told her that was accurate? – the ten provinces, the harshness of the winter, the four seasons, Quebec in ferment? – but as the uniformity of all airports in the world prevents individuality, Maya had quickly found a bus on the international terminal access road and had taken a seat in it under the false certitude that nothing had changed. But beyond that, the lines were blurred. And what did she see? As far as her eyes could reach stretched roads, squat houses, and a land scarred by the cold. And farther away? Nothing. They had forgotten to tell her that one does not come into a country on equal footing, that the work of decoding was slow and that the obstacles to emigration were difficult to overcome, that one must not be taken in by the snares of a tourist experience, that there are new countries similar to coastal seas dotted with treacherous islands and contrary currents.

Saint Henri Square. Now she is face to face with Jean-Lou to whom she must give an account. He is waiting there, in the pale light of the neon signs, lost in the hugeness of this school of thick lines. What could she tell him?

In the grip of a new claustrophobia, she is now going

from door to door, from street to street, searching for a way out. She retains the hope that she will meet someone. After all, those long detours and the silent alienation of this place could easily be dissipated The appearance of a colleague accustomed to the maze of the *polyvalente* or of a concierge appearing out of an office in business attire, armed with important bunches of keys, both possessed with a peace that they had stolen from her and for which she is fighting and is distracted, panting and already conquered. She is easy prey for the overwhelming images of terrifying phantoms that require a new language of her.

The class is one solid team, and the students look at each other. They do not care about the G.N.P., the return value, business costs, the production process, or the price index; they are not interested in the facts of the problem or the possibilities area or even the price of tea or the price of coffee. These were feigned commodities, useless information, inconveniences. The noise increases more and more, sound inflation, despotism.

Meanwhile the diagram and the table from page twelve take form on the chalkboard under her fingers, and the words, the words alone, explain the evolution of the nominal and real gross national product, unless it is a nominal or real evolution; but how would she, who is learning her subject but is unable to teach it, know? The room explodes unavoidably and suddenly vibrates under the light. The class is now a playground where fantasy is the only referee. Without discipline or guilt, the students dash, collide, talk, and yell; their cries of liberation dominate the classroom. The word, like a bullet, completes its trajectory and, in its flight, reaches the speakers; there it ricochets, virulent, mulitiplied, culminating, while isolated

Maya stops speaking and explaining, because the class is no longer listening to her.

For a moment, panic-stricken, as if having lost the reins, she watches the students who left her before she even realized what was happening. She tries to control the class using her prestige as a teacher whose value lies in her authority, her power, her sarcasm, and her good manners, but the students pay no attention to her. They left in a blue, reddish or turquoise train, it makes no difference, an immense amusement train that runs without announcing the stations, without whistling, without worrying, and without knitting its eyebrows. Beside this train, Maya is nothing more than a station platform, a secondary route, a grade crossing that leaves no impression on the memory of the travelers, as long as it is bare, drab, and bereft of mystery. Then, partly from countenance, partly from tactic, she does a turnabout and the supervisor disappears. She takes a place with the students in the amusement train; she joins in unwillingly and plays their game. Instinctually, she finds the one needed gesture, because the students, shocked, look at her. For one moment she regains the lead, but she quickly senses that the ensuing crossfire of clever witticisms further isolates her in her singularity. In that moment she begins to question her prestige, her duty, and the value of her purpose; and failure, fear, guilt over a poorly done job, anguish in anticipation of the coming day, and the terror of needing to justify herself – of confronting the gray, keen, sharp, prying eyes of the administration and the principal – take shape again.

Now, the class watches as Carole or Sylvie or Manon wrestle with Jaques, rolling to and fro with passion. They describe them with words that Maya does not understand. Meanwhile, Diane and Raymonde laugh and their laughter bounces off the walls, and Manon spreads her legs while her boots give her the look of a Cossack and her laugh penetrates everywhere, even under the short tweed skirt that is now open like the flesh offered as a challenge, a provocation.

Maya has not seen the last of embarrassing surprises. There are the words whose meanings escape her and the gestures and the sign made with the index finger that Monique or Francine or Marc uses to summon her and which shocks her because, without a doubt, she falls into the trap of her only possible reference, her own culture. There is the disparity between this gesture (because it is informal there and one uses it to emphasize a difference in class) and the gravity of the accompanying look. Apprenticeship on the heap. Was this really the only way for an immigrant teacher to know the children of this new country? Who does the erroneous interpretation benefit? Why so much disappointed energy, so many misguided glances? Should they not have told her about this aspect of her job, of which she is ignorant and for which she has no experience – this decoding of communication signs that are not really identical to her own? But no – the misunderstanding continues, each party denying the evidence.

The horseplay becomes more serious. Maya feels the ground give way beneath her. Her powerlessness is great, and her anger as well, as in the face of a dead end or a sudden obstruction. She clearly sees the impassable abyss that opens up, and there is something tragic in the idea that the image that she has of herself no longer has the slightest correlation to the image she gets from the students' feedback. She had counted on a rich, fertile past, and now it betrays her and runs aground like an oceanliner on the beach.

The students, however, do not see the image of the

oceanliner, no more than they see the rich, fertile past. What they have before their eyes is more like a drifting derelict or even a look of distress, the annulation of the expert, without dignity, without power, and without words. It is a wall of refusal that the class sets up against Maya.

For the fourth time, the intersection – at least if this is not a different one, but how could she know when confronted with this same invariable horizon? Feverish, she hastens her pace, scrutinizes the names of the streets, and plunges down Maisonneuve, high society in colors, at the end of which a wall in perspective lets one see a pale sun, softened by blue and neon rays. And her expectation, like a sure instinct, forces her to continue: on the left, the opening of another corridor. Du Clocher Street.

The *polyvalente* had not been able to receive the blow. Nevertheless, it had included a cafeteria, around fifty classrooms, two auditoriums, an amphitheater, and six workshops. It was in charge of, that is to say, everything besides the science, the culture, and the Socialization, it supplied the food, the electricity, the air-conditioning, the ventilation (but not the ionization of the air), the vastness, and the three strident notes of the bell at the end of class – but three thousand students are a lot! "It is for this reason that your child is enrolled in the afternoon school," specified the flier sent to the parents. "Classes will begin at 1:00 pm and will end at 6:00 pm." Then they specified the number of classes, the daily schedule . . .

Now it is break time, which lasts for half an hour. It is late afternoon, at sunset. But what is the good of talking about sky and light since they had forgotten to include them in the décor? Mrs. Roy is in the hallway. She supervises the flow of the students who are leaving class.

Maya is in the classroom without being there, to tell the truth. Her body and her hands repeat the same movements over and over again as if, by concentrating on nothing but going through the motions of tidying up, she was taking refuge in a ritual that exorcised her and transported her beyond the daily routine. It is a short, privileged moment when she is able to forget, along with the disrespect of the students, her powerlessness to establish some kind of communication with them. Now she finds herself in Mrs. Roy's optical field, but not by chance. The latter knows very well where her steps are going and that Maya constitutes for the vice-principal a hub around which each of her steps are going to gravitate in a sort of irresistible spiral, centripetal force, that pushes them towards each other, one against the other, but of which neither the one nor the other is fully aware.

And in the long, half-lit, tunnel-like hallway she advances, the Vice-Principal, her face and body impassive and even rigid, as if frozen in the halo of her duty. Without difficulty, she occupies the center of things. To her, this hallway is nothing but a space to supervise, a place where she will tame, as if by a miracle, the dash of the student and the gesture of the professor.

Mrs. Roy is a prototype, a guardian of discipline, a defender of the precarious order. A student – Yvan Lamontagne – breaks the rules. He crosses the hallway and stops suddenly in front of her. There she is on the edge of her anger, as if enlarged by her task. Her eyes of steel and her forehead of steel, and her nerves of steel, and her finger of steel simultaneously express the signs before which the student bows, makes a U-turn, and disappears.

One moment, she checks to see that the doors of the

classrooms are shut, retraces her steps in the direction of Maya, her pace deliberate and slow, an obvious sign of her place in the hierarchy.

The distance between them shrinks. Maya would like to change the transparence of her own features, to wash them of their agitation and to assume before Mrs. Roy, who is getting closer and closer, the face that she puts on every morning. She could have, she would have been able to go down quickly, before the concierge shuts the doors of the department. But it is too early to make herself a mask and too late to avoid the encounter. And why should she avoid it? Did she not owe an account to the vice-principal? Was it not she who had given her, on October 20th, this position as a full-time substitute in TC 21? Besides, had they not told her that it was on the basis of this woman's recommendation, and only on the basis of her recommendation, that she would have the position as a teacher? Several times she had felt, although very mitigated, a sympathy that comforted her. Perhaps after all, she needed to talk to her today about even her difficulty in teaching a subject that she did not know, but Maya feels reluctant. She needs to back away to see clearly within herself, to understand, to associate her links that seemed scattered to her.

Through the open door, Maya sees the vice-principal on level with the second vault, the one which opens onto Maisonneuve Street, across from the stairs. There are no longer more than several meters separating them. Since Maya had finished tidying up the classroom, there is nothing left to do but turn around. The employer – or almost – and the employee are then face to face.

Sciences Street. Disabled, Maya looks around her. Is this the fifth time that she emerges into the square? Unless it is another one with the same narrow streets and the same horizon interrupted by sections of walls. Will there be a way out soon, an open door, an escape to the outside?

Maya immediately feels the disapproval in the tone of the vice-principal. She speaks slowly, from the height of her prestige. Words, a plethora of words, cross the thin, dry lips, whistle like bullets around them, and strike the walls of the empty classroom where the power of the one intensifies to the detriment of the other.

Maya does not have the time to respond. The flood of words, although slowly and thoughtlessly repeated, do not leave room for a reply. There are several silences during which she could have entered the discussion but she feels the incongruity of such action on her part and, deep within her, the validity of the reproaches that are directed at her. How can she deny the indeniable? Mrs. Roy coldly outlines the disciplinary situation in TC 21. She interprets Maya's difficulty with her group as evidence of her incompetence. With a movement of her head, she underlines her incomprehensible passivity, with lightning in her voice she grieves over the weakness by which Maya allows herself to be invaded and her powerlessness to maintain the leadership.

Maya is speechless, vulnerable, and without defense before the criticism. They had, however, told her about the administration's rigid adherence to the strictest discipline; they had described to her the domineering personality of Mrs. Roy; they had even advised her to avoid all dispute with the administration, to solve her problems with the class herself, to never involve the vice-principals, the severe watchdogs of order for order. It does not matter that this order hides a certain disorder, or that it is a sign of totalitarianism, the unilateral power of the teacher, or pretense, or the result of dubious compromise. Disconcerted, Maya realises – she for whom competence at teaching is no longer something to be proved – that she must again take up arms and fight and defend herself and assert herself and look for other ways to convince, to charm, and to reduce the misgivings. Will they give her the time – the time for a return to herself, the time for a de-conditioning?

Does Maya not know that her past must no longer serve as a point of reference for her, that she, the thirty-year-old, the immigrant with a successful career as a biology teacher, with six years of experience, ambitious, selected by the Canadian immigration department, hand-picked, and finally chosen by virtue of her past, had to renounce this past, to die to one form and be reborn in another, like the child who dies to become an adult and the adult who dies to become an old person? Does Maya not know that it is necessary to lose everything in order to gain everything? For the moment, bound hand and foot, she is delivered to the court where Mrs. Roy presides. Mrs. Roy indicts her for a lack of authority, denies her all teaching qualities, judges her inept at teaching, and suddenly, changing her mind, grants her a reprieve, alleging that she has not had a chance to prove herself, that one month of teaching "is not long enough to draw conclusions," that the title of substitute obviously lacks prestige, that the students take advantage of this situation, and that the lack of security in which Maya lives is a serious handicap, but that however, discipline is fundamental; discipline makes the teacher; discipline makes the school.

But the words, all the words are gestures. Round, precise, they mark out the place that defines us. And their place is not the same. Mrs. Roy launched her voice from the high places of authority. It was a form of imperialism of power with which she was, she herself, invested and which gave her an advantage over the other. Maya, she, took refuge in the back country of her illusions, of her choices, of a past that she was reproducing without doubting it and which is also a form of imperialism of the culture. And these two beings were confronting one another in an untenable position.

Maya does not at all recover from this mess. Mrs. Roy reduces her in pieces and she, dumbfounded, no longer recognizes herself in the debris, a broken puzzle that one holds up for her like a mirror. She feels rejected, hopelessly lost.

Mrs. Roy continues, unperturbed. From the point of her smile, she announces to Maya a change of position. She will be relieved of full-time substitution. Her classes, they would give them to another, a specialist in "commercial transactions." "I fully understand," says Maya, "and to be frank, it's even a relief for me."

Although her sincerity is evident, she suddenly feels that it is unwelcome and even interpreted by Mrs. Roy as another one of her incapabilities. And Mrs. Roy continued that there would always be time to leave teaching but that, at any rate, they sometimes needed part-time substitutes. As for recommendations to the schoolboards, she will do nothing for the moment, waiting for an improvement, a considerable one, she specified, in Maya's work.

"First of all, the students must accept you," she adds while moving away toward the east of the *polyvalente* where students already gather to escape the noise of the public square.

There she is, Maya, outside of the circuit. They had put her on a path of escape, out of order, like the imported mechanical reapers that are scrapped because the manufacturer had forgotten to translate the instruction manual into the language of the country.

Maya had stretched herself out on the pavement, past the stage of being hurt, broken and alone. There is not the slightest way out in sight. Hope had fled, little by little, over the same horizon interrupted by sections of walls. Des Érables Avenue. Her anxiety mounts and growls and increases in volume and gets caught among the concrete pillars. Are these not the same ones that she encounters for the sixth or seventh time?

A door opens on the past . . . A post card past, a frozen past, a past fixed but sumptuous, embroidered with gold and light, with the harsh midday light that floats on the sea. There is the summer house. It opens on all sides to the summer which surrounds it and fills it with the luxurious aromas of its vegetation. Her heart beats to the rhythm of the seasons. It punctuates life with little steps, and the days of childhood crumble at the liking of the innocense-bearing wind: flavor of golden honey, of molasses gorged with brown gold, bearer of life.

Standing before the summer, leaning her elbows on the blue crossroads of the morning, Maya gathers the first gust of warmth that rises from the earth like an offering. Soon, she will go down and, while the house fills with the smells of mixed spices, of ground cumin, of crushed corriander, of pressed garlic, of sesame butter, while the flavors of the tomato and of the parsley and of the onion exhude in the process of cooking, and while the melted butter will permeate the rice, the crushed wheat, or the green beans, she will go towards the arbor at the end of the garden, to the shade of the ficus tree. Intoxication rises from the earth, Mother Earth, beloved, lover, incestuous.

At the end of the path, the supple and delicate stems of

the jasmine stand watch up to the window up there. The mornings of these vacations are dotted with a thousand perennial and white and delicate little flowers like the star-fish that never die on the mother-stem but which fall and survive long after. These are the flowers of memory because, immortal, their perfume survives a long time, tenacious, after their passage, subtle, after their death.

It is a morning in the month of June. Maya opens the shutters and slips into the countryside. And through the partly opened neck of her blouse and under the rolled up sleeves and in the hollow of her hips and along her bare legs, she inspects with the tip of her fingers the pulpy flesh of summer while the breeze listlessly rocks the blue branches of the jacaranda and while the delicate corolla of a hollyhock opens under her window . . . an uncultivated garden, a still-palpable presence, a witness of her past.

The summer mornings drop one by one, like clear notes, crystalline, intact, and identical to one another. They hum with the thousand voices of life: customary voices, peaceful voices, puerile or raucous voices, dissonant or serious, or deep, or discordant, or resounding, or soft, or intense, or joyful and harmonious and singing.

There is the serious and modulated clamor, the inviting call of the fruit vendor going from one corner to another and pulling, with his robust arms, a cart filled with overflowing crates, rich with colors and contrasts, a vivid palette of luminous and simultaneous tones. With each weighing of vegetables and with each fall back, there is the clash of the weighing pans, of the needle and the beam and of the weights clinking, like so many vibrating sounds, escaped from multiple percussion instruments in a country festival. There is the three-note call, the singular voice of the travel-

ing craftsman, braiding straw, restorer of seats, master up-
holsterer, making his living at the whims of fortune. And,
suddenly, harsh, sprung up from the corridor of the street,
the hurried, nervous, impatient chime of the electric tram-
way, shaking its creaking metal carcass. Then the hour soars
aloft from the minarets like a mournful wail: time-out for the
tumultuous city.

And the traditional bells of the herd of goats ring, a form
of live advertising, an eloquent message, instant information
on the product, the quality, the place of the sale, and the
available quantity.

When the evening tames the day, a new language will be
born, a nocturnal language of the breeze mingled with the
human hum, a tide rising until the wee hours of the morning,
unstable and alive, a seeker of salubrious shade and quiet.

Then the river rises. Its two banks overflow with mud
and river deposits, black earth set with gold and life and
promises and toil and fruit.

A childish voice, a brief song, wanders through the
streets, offering the perfume of jasmine or of camelia in
exchange for any merchandise. And this voice loses itself in
the eddies of the river, a fragile ripple, clothed with dancing
clusters of little star-flowers, lavish in imperishable ecstasy
and abundant happiness. So the child-vendor, although poor
and modest, becomes the merchant of rapturous emotion
and intoxication and illusions, embroidering with gold the
perfumed air of memory.

*Translated from the French by Sharon Hathaway*

# ABLA FARHOUD

## DOUNIA-A-WORLD

CHAPTER ONE

I told my children: "When the day comes I can't manage on
my own, put me in a nursing home." They replied: "No,
never, you are our mother; we'll take care of you."

With age, we confuse resignation with wisdom, which is
why I went on: "When a baby is born, he is laid in a cradle
until he outgrows it; when old people get too old, they are
put in a home in a crib with iron bars until they are ready to
die. Every country has its customs, and there is nothing
wrong with that, the result is the same. That is the cycle of
life. I have lived what I was meant to live and I can die
without disturbing anyone . . . A peasant who is self-suffi-
cient ignores that he is a sultan . . ."

The words escaped from my mouth, clear and organized, with only a slight hesitation that has become natural to
me with time. I rarely say so much at once and I felt the
excitement of a child eating the first ice cream cone of the
summer after a long winter.

Although my children kept saying "no, never," each in
their own way, in Arabic or French or with a gesture like
Farid who grunts rather than speaks, I sensed they were
relieved. Salim, my husband, shook his head and raised his

eyes, sighing as he always does when he is offended. He had struck the expression "nursing home" from his vocabulary long ago and, just feeling his glance toward me, I know he resented my opening this door. Myriam said nothing and just watched the scene unfold as she usually does. Then Abdullah, my eldest, stood up and declared vehemently: "Never, Mother, I'll never let you go. You've taken care of us all your life. I'll take care of you."

There was a short pause. Even the children of my children turned to stare at their uncle.

All of us knew that Abdullah could not take care of me. When the raptor bird comes to feed inside his head, when he is lost and dispossessed, what can he do for me, my gentle Abdullah, when he can do nothing for himself?

We were at Samira's, my oldest daughter who had invited us for Sunday dinner and a family photo sitting. For once, no one was missing. It has never been easy to get us all together for a few hours; there's always at least one who's sick or on a trip or busy. Samira, the main organizer of the family, and Kaokab, the youngest, have often tried to gather everyone for a family portrait before their father and I left this world. In our last and only picture, Kaokab is a toddler and Samira a young girl.

That day the photographer didn't show up and Samira was so distressed she said fate was against us. Really, to speak of fate for such a trivial matter . . .

I was a little sad as I ate. Just a little sad. Is that why I mentioned the nursing home? I think an old woman should never be allowed to drink wine . . .

I sensed it was the end to something. I had the feeling it was the last time I would have a meal with all my loved ones gathered together.

In the waning phase of life, with or without wine, we often feel the end to something. One day you can't climb the stairs without losing your breath, one day you can't climb at all; one day you can't sit on the floor or get up without help; one day you can't eat the hot pepper you adore, one day you can't eat anything without getting indigestion, one day a tooth is pulled, then another, until you're left with a mouth you don't even recognize; one day you can no longer kiss a child without wiping your mouth first, one day you look in the mirror and you see a woman who might have been your grandmother.

Ah, youth, if you were to return one day, I would tell you what age has made of me . . .

Little pieces of yourself leave, as distinctly as small lights snuffed out. You can see it, you can feel it. This strange body that has become yours, however you try to tame it, continues to change and deteriorate until the end. We mourn the loss of little pieces of ourselves well before our children mourn our passing.

Age is considerate enough to proceed step by step, entering gently day by day. Otherwise we would never be able to accept it or learn to say that as long as we are alive, as long as our children and grand children are alive, the rest is of no importance. As the body ages, the value of things changes in our mind. And that's as it should be.


I looked at each of them, one after another, without their noticing me, concerned as they were about this photographer who won't come, quickly forgetting the nursing home that will come one day.

Salim, my husband, throned at the head of the table. As

usual, he talked and waved his hands about, and I said nothing, I listened. Samira, my eldest daughter, moved in and out of the dining room, nimble and self-assured, her gestures precise and economical. Everything must be perfect. Every object in her house has its place and everything must be put back where it belongs. All the houses I've lived in were always topsy-turvy in spite of my best efforts to correct this. Samira's husband is as rich as she is and they have no children. I have six children and five grandchildren and they are the only wealth I have. My second daughter, Myriam, has two children, Véronique and David. I go to her place most often, because of the children. She writes books. I only know how to write my name. Kaokab, my youngest, is the one person I know who can whip her father in an oral debate or a contest of funny stories. When she is there, Salim listens more often than he speaks, which is a remarkable feat. Kaokab is a language professor. I barely speak even in my own language and know but a few words in French and English. Samir, the youngest of the boys, has three children: Amélie, Julien, and Gabriel. I can't imagine when he found the time to make them. Maybe in a plane. That's where he met his wife. One day in Hong Kong, the next in Brazil or Chili. I don't know where these countries are exactly, just that they're far from here. My son Farid has no children but he has a dozen jobs. Often, he designs and makes furniture. I like to draw birds. And then there's Abdullah, the eldest of the family; he has neither wife nor children.

My gaze moved back and forth from one to the other and I couldn't help asking myself if these were really my children or maybe the neighbors' brood, as they say.

Sitting beside Kaokab was a man I had seen a few times. Next to Farid was a woman I had never seen before. Farid and Kaokab never stay too long with the same person. I figure whatever makes them happy, very well. My husband has a hard time accepting this. Despite the many years we've lived in this country, the customs still seem unthinkable to him. Especially when it comes to his daughters. Good Lord! the speeches I had to hear about Quebecois, Canadian, American society when Myriam broke up with her husband. Salim was not interested in my reminding him that divorce was not invented here, that people do divorce in Lebanon, even more since the war, that customs change everywhere, not just here. He would not listen. He was enraged rather than pained. He wound up saying the world was rushing to its end and that life makes no sense. He always finishes his speech with this phrase. Then he goes to bed and sleeps to get strength back or to forget.

We were all sorry to lose Myriam's husband; we liked him very much, even if he didn't speak our language. He was so good with Abdullah during his bad moments. All I said to Myriam was "Dear, you know children need a father." She replied, "Their father isn't dead. They'll live with him every other week." This struck my heart so painfully. I could see them with their suitcases trodding from their mother's to their father's house with never a home of their own. All I said was "Are you sure their father can feed them properly?" Her eyes were all puffy; she must have been crying a lot. "Mother, all you think about is food. There's more to life than just eating. But don't worry, their father is a really good cook." I thought "a mother can never be replaced," but I didn't say anything, I didn't want to add to her suffering. I'm not very good with words; I don't know how to speak. I leave that to Salim. I know how to feed people.

My words are sprigs of parsley that I wash, green clusters that I pull off the stem and chop, peppers and courgettes that I empty out to stuff better, potatoes that I peel, grape vine and cabbage leaves that I roll.

For over fifty years I have prepared food and every time it's different. I improve the dishes, I invent new recipes, new ways of cooking sometimes. I wonder if words are that different. Sometimes I use a spoon to mix, but often I really enjoy plunging my hands into the bowl. My clean, bare hands touch the food my children will eat. This is how I can do them good. I can't do much else, but I know how to do that.

It is very rare that Salim or the children thank me. This has never bothered me. Do you say thank you when someone says "I love you?" You can answer "I love you too" but you don't say thank you.

Sometimes I would like to be able to speak, with words. As time went by I forgot how. But in the past ten years, I've occasionally tried. The words come out all unraveled. Little pieces stay stuck inside and nobody understands what I'm trying to say. Even I find it all mixed up. I can see that what is in my head has nothing to do with what comes out of my mouth. So I keep quiet. The worst is when I'm trying to tell a story that I know well, something that happened to me. When Salim is there he'll start the whole story over. He takes his time, rounding out his words, giving all the details, even those I'd forgotten or thought weren't important. He stands up, finds just the right gestures to flesh out his phrases, to bring the tale to life. Everybody is hanging on his words. Including me. Suddenly this simple little story takes on importance. Even for me who was there. I don't know how he does it. I envy him. I admire him too.

Yet I remember, when I was little, I used to talk. I knew how to talk. Unlike my sister, always quiet, I talked. I said what I thought. I made my father and my brothers and sisters laugh. My father's guests too. One day I even made Mahmoud Boutrabi laugh; he was known in the whole village for his sour personality and lack of humor. No one had ever seen him smile, much less actually laugh. My father noticed my feat and I became known as the girl who had succeeded in making Mahmoud Boutrabi laugh. I wasn't afraid to make people face their own truths, which made everybody else laugh. I left no stone unturned. It was easy then, so easy.

What happened to make my words turn into wheat kernels, grains of rice, grape leaves and cabbage leaves? My thoughts into olive oil and lemon juice? When did it start? It could not be Salim who forced this change. I was so quick to leave my place to him, to lose my tongue to his, that it must have started long before. But when?

I'm sure the meal must have been very good. I ate with a lost appetite. As always when Samira invites us, she complained we were eating too fast, that it was not worth cooking for hours on end to devour it all in five minutes. She's right of course, but why bother repeating this since no words have ever changed a jot of this bad habit.

Salim is the one who always responds to Samira's remarks. He says it's hereditary, that our ancestors had to eat in the same big dish in the middle of the table and each had to swallow as fast as possible if they wanted to satisfy their hunger; he says when he first came here he never had the time to finish his plate because customers came into the store at all hours and that since his children worked in his stores they also had to eat fast. He always winds up saying he eats fast because he hates cold food. Old people always tell the same stories. I'd rather keep quiet.

I don't know what came over me and made me talk. To tell my children to put me in a nursing home . . . I'd rather die. Why talk about that now?

I have good children, they'll take care of me, I'm sure, but how can you be sure of anything? One bad deed can erase all previous good deeds from memory. To forget is human. That's what human means. Ingratitude is the most common of faults . . .

. . . My heart reaches out to the heart of my child but my child's heart is a stone . . . Parents are devoted to their children and they in turn are devoted to their own children. It's the natural order.

It is very hard to keep an old woman in the house, I know, I took care of Salim's grandmother for two years before her death . . .

Each has his own life. My daughters have their work and my sons . . . Oh, Lord, why rehash all that now?

Most of all, I'm worried about Abdullah. Who will look after him when his father and I are gone? If my children are willing to send their mother to a nursing home, will they leave their brother in the street?

I'm sure everything will turn out all right. I am healthy, thank God, I can come and go and cook. I take after my father who lived to ninety-five with almost all his teeth and all his wits. Why do I worry before the time comes? They say . . . the bark feels soft only to the tree it surrounds . . . With my six children and five grandchildren, I have eleven layers of bark surrounding me.

CHAPTER 4

Myriam wanted to drive me home. I said I would enjoy the walk. I let myself be persuaded more easily in winter. Walking is treacherous, especially when the ice hides under the snow. I used to love to climb over the snow banks on the curbs . . . Myriam and the children wanted me to stay for supper and sleep over. I had nothing ready for Salim and he doesn't like to eat alone. I didn't tell Myriam this, she would have said her father was a grown man and it was time for me to think about myself a bit. Easier said than done.

I muttered something about having to uncover the yogurt I'd started, so it wouldn't get too sour. In fact the yogurt could have waited, I could have made labneh, that's even better. But I wanted to leave. I made Véronique and David promise to come for lunch the next day to give their mother a little break, and I left with no regrets, I'll see them tomorrow.

Even though I walk less and less, I love to walk. I think about a time when I will no longer be able to. I like this neighborhood where I've lived since I fled Lebanon. If I count right, I lived near thirty years in Lebanon and some forty in Canada. Since I've gotten old, I have time to rethink, to count over, but I never get the same result. I lived in Chagour, the village I was born in, until I married Samir; then I moved to his village Bir Barra; the first time we immigrated in the fifties, we stayed about fifteen years, returned to Lebanon some ten years. When the war broke out, we came back to Canada.

I must have counted wrong . . . I lived longer over there than here . . . I think.

For me, here or there, it's all the same. If my children

were over there, that's where I'd live; since they're home here, so am I. The only difference is the climate. Calmer here because of the snow, more joyful there because of the sun.

For a long time any sun or joy was snatched away from us. For a long time people turned into enemies of others and war remained the enemy of all.

Death and suffering is what makes us all human, although often I think some hardly deserve to be called human. A child who has been killed, whether from a rich or a poor family, whether from a friendly or an enemy clan, remains a dead child. And the torment of those who stay behind, women or men, rich or poor, here or there, is the same. I think death unites us and life separates us. Life reveals our differences, death our resemblances. In life everyone needs to show his power and mark his territory; in death there is no power or territory. Not even a marble headstone can change that. Your friend's body rots as quickly as your enemy's. Nothing looks more like a dead person than another dead person. Vanity is the realm of the living. Death is identical for all and it amounts to a breath that is snuffed out.

It's odd how war on the outside can distract us from the war on the inside. When death is waiting at the door, everything else loses its importance. The petty simply fades away. Only the essential remains: how to avoid getting killed, how to eat and drink, how to laugh too in spite of it all.

Approaching death, an entire life amounts to a blink, an eye opening, an eye closing and it's over.

I am going to sit a while to rest. My knees can hardly bear my body. At times, I can hardly bear it myself. When my grandchildren were little, they'd tell me, "You beautiful Sitto." This pleased me even though I didn't believe them. Children, like lovers, see with the heart.

When I was a little girl, I would wash my face over and over, I would scrub it so that it would turn white. It got all red instead. If it hadn't been for how others saw me, I would perhaps have found my face attractive, smooth and clear as I washed it. In those days it didn't seem to make much difference if men were dark or fair, but women were expected to be white and round. I grew up round but stayed brown.

I spent many years convinced that no one could see me. My mother was busy feeding us and making coffee for all my father's visitors. He was busy talking to others, trying to restore peace in their hearts. When I was little, there were already endless killings going on among the French and the Druze, and my father, who was neither French nor Druze, did his best to stop the blood flow. He believed in the power of words and coffee helps to talk.

Much later my husband was busy making money so we could survive, busy watching other women he found more attractive, busy with his frustrations too. He had a lot to deal with.

My eyes opened and soon they will close forever. It all

goes too quickly. I have not had the time to force people to see me. I tried too often.

As time went by I learned you can't force anything. What happens happens. We look at those we love. That's all there is to it.

I wanted him to look at me and to say "Dounia, you're beautiful, I love you." But maybe it wasn't even possible at the time I needed it. Tenderness . . . even today, a tender look rushes through my body and flows out of my eyes. Age has not helped to change this. Salim is the same. Like me, he is an orphan. He lost his father very young, and worse, his mother never loved him. I can not imagine a mother would dislike her child. It's perhaps because she barely knew him and didn't raise him. Salim was living in Lebanon and his mother in Canada. He was already thirty years old when they met again. And my mother-in-law had just lived through an inhuman tragedy: the illness and death of her daughter. There was no place for anything except her pain. When I think of all she put us through, I am tempted to hate her, but then I remember what happened to her and I forgive her.

Salim and I were orphans . . . He lost his father; I lost my mother . . . Two orphans hungry for tenderness and affection who get married bring into the world children with no parents, I think, orphans like them, beggars, because an orphan can never become wholly a father or a mother. Everything is always off balance. Lack is the twin brother of abundance.

Rich people say, "Marry the poor, multiply beggars." Their disdain used to shock me and still does, but I know now that poverty is not what we think, nor is true wealth, which has nothing to do with goods we stock and count.

True wealth is there or not, it leaves without warning and returns on a whim. We can not draw pride or vanity from it. We carry it in us without recognizing it until the day we lose it. A small spark, so small we have not yet discovered its name . . .

Neither Salim nor myself were ever considered poor where we were born. Far from that. Salim owned land and his mother sent him money from Canada. He lived without laboring, like a sheik. As for me, I was the daughter of the priest, our family also received money from overseas, and we owned land.

I think Salim was in love with me. He must have loved me, otherwise why did he come up to visit us so often? It was a good two hour walk from his village to ours. He must have found me attractive, although he never said so, or why would he have asked for my hand? You don't marry an ugly girl just because she's the daughter of the most respected priest in the region. He could have asked for my sister, but no, he wanted to marry me.

Any girl from our region would have been proud to marry him. He was handsome, fair-skinned with thick black hair, he was strong, he feared nothing, he had money. And he knew how to talk, Lord, was he a good talker. And a marvelous story teller. He could make a foreigner forget his home country. He captured us with old tales and new ones he invented. No one ever got bored when he was around. The smallest anecdote became a tale of A Thousand and One Nights, sometimes funny, sometimes frightening, always fascinating. He made me laugh a lot. And cry too.

Salim needed people around him. Lots of people. It

seemed he would do anything to be liked. And he was always likeable when there was company around. He was so different when our house was full from when it was empty, with just me and the children . . . He used to head for the village square when there was no one around the house to talk with or listen to his stories. In Canada there was no village square, no ears ready to soak up his words, no eyes to see him, no one to understand his stories. Here everybody works all day, then goes home. He had to work all day too. Here men go to the neighborhood tavern to drink beer and watch television. Salim had no taste for beer or for television. Even though he could get along in the language here, it wouldn't do. A story teller needs to master a language better than any. Even his children, who might have become his audience, gradually forgot their father's language or lost interest as they got older.

Locked in his throat, his stories were choking him.

The first years we lived here, both of us were suffocating. He grew desperate looking to the outside world and I grew desperate looking at him. His pain burst out in blows, breaking everything and everyone he touched. And mine was bursting inside with no way to let it out.

We might have smothered to death had it not been for the children. They saved us I think.

My first child born in Canada nested in the place of this pain, took the breath I was struggling to let out. She began growing in my belly soon after I got here. She took everything. It's too much for a child. I did not want her to live. May God forgive me, but I will never forgive myself.

When I think of this child I resentfully carried, I wonder by what miracle did Kaokab survive, by what grace can she smile, talk, laugh?

Destiny's paths are incomprehensible at the moment we take them, or later for that matter.

Is that a fig tree I see in the grocer's window? It wasn't there this morning . . . The Greek has managed to grow a fig tree in his garden and brought it to his store to keep him company . . . My God, what work it takes to hold onto something. To escape the suffering of loss. To keep the past alive. The Greek smiles at me. He must have seen my astonishment and points at his little fig tree to say yes, it's real. He is so proud of it . . . how long it takes to break away.

To immigrate, to leave, leave everything behind that you will soon start calling mine: my sun, my water, my fruits, my plants, my trees, my village. When you're in your home village, you never say my sun. It's just the sun, and why talk about it since it's always there and always has been. You don't say my village, you simply live there. Everything is habit, even your faith. I realized this when I left my home to live in my husband's village.

The other day I told Abdullah that I immigrated the first time when I married and went to live in Bir Barra. He laughed. For him to immigrate is to leave your country, to cross oceans, to go to the end of the earth. Yet he recalled it is said that the Prophet Mohammed emigrated from Mecca to Medina, two cities in the same region where the same language is spoken. I don't know if the Prophet felt like an immigrant, but I know that I did. Because it was when moving from my village to my husband's that I began to make comparisons, to see differences, to experience loss and nostalgia, to long to be elsewhere but incapable of going, to feel like a foreigner.

For me it was like another country. Even though you could walk the distance between the two villages, people were so different, and for them I was different. I was a foreigner who had stolen Salim from some likely marriage to a girl from the village. My accent was not theirs, they didn't like what I did, and I didn't like what they did. The fruit and the vegetables did not have the same taste, their priest was not my father, their landscape was not the one I had known. Their village was surrounded by mountains; it was hotter and the air was heavier. My village stood on a high peak and I felt I could see to the end of the earth. Since the end of my childhood, I have never again gazed at the horizon. In my husband's village the mountains shut off the view; in Montreal, as in Beirut, the buildings block the view.

The only advantage was the water. The village well was two steps from the house and we were allowed to draw two buckets a day, sometimes three. When I was little I had to walk for miles to fill a pitcher, but how delicious the water was . . . maybe I was just tired from the hike. Here it's even better. You just open the faucet. The faucet is a marvel and forty years later I still experience the thrill of that first miraculous moment when I turned on the tap and clear water flowed over my hands. Even today I sometimes stop and raise my eyes to heaven in thanks.

CHAPTER 16

There are some things you can't say, that should never be spoken even to yourself, that should be banished from your thoughts.

There are things that return in spite of your efforts to hold them back, sour and bitter like vomit you swallow again; there are violent things that you would rather see as madness, a lapse of reasoning, but that you still can not forget or forgive.

There are things that carry the weight of all our fears, of all our cowardliness.

There are things we are so ashamed we can not speak them even in a whisper. There is shame that is not eased by time, things we can not forgive ourselves or ever erase. Shame that remains as vivid as the day it began.

I am ashamed . . . I have been ashamed for fifty years. I writhe in shame just remembering it.

I can still hear my father's voice, I hear it as clearly as I see that dusty boot coming toward me and smashing into my face.

I see my father turning away from me disdainfully.

My father and the father of my children were sitting on their horses, preparing to leave. I said, "Salim, please don't go, the baby is due any day, I don't want to be alone like the last two." That's all I said. What harm was there in asking this man whom I had chosen as husband, who had chosen me as his wife, that no one had forced me to marry, this man that I loved, what harm was there in asking him to stay in the village for the birth of his third child?

This was not the first time he had raised his hand to hit me, but it was the first time he dared in front of my father, the most respected priest of the region, and with his foot, a boot across the face, you wouldn't even kick a dog that way.

From the height of his horse my father saw everything.

My father, the one I thought my father and protector, did not move. Not a gesture, not a word to support me, to defend me, to show this man who had just ripped my lip open that I was not fatherless, that I had a family, that I had to be treated with respect.

Nothing. Not the slightest gesture, not a word, not a glimmer of reproach. Nothing.

I was the one to be blamed. He spit the words in my face: "Damned be those who brought you into the world."

This was the worst insult. In front of the man who had humiliated me, instead of defending me, he cursed me. He cursed my birth, my entire being, the day and the person who had given me life. My father, whom I held above all else, whom I honored and loved, damned me because I was weak.

Where could I run to? Where could I escape? Where could I go? If my father scorned me and looked the other way, where could I go?

At the moment my father turned away from me and cursed me, I felt alone, so alone. A nail without a head . . .

My back bone crumbled at that second . . .

Humiliated by my husband, with no support from my father, with two small children and a third on its way, full of shame . . . where could I go?

Even today, fifty years later, I ask myself why did I not flee, why did I do nothing?

I was not capable of betraying the father who had just betrayed me, of making him live the shame of a daughter without a husband or a home. I was not raised that way. Because I had been raised to respect this father who had stooped to insulting the memory of my mother, the woman who had borne a daughter who let her mouth be torn open. Because we were raised to respect and honor our father, our brothers, our husband, and to depend on the protection of men. Because this father and this whole community of men and women taught us to bend, to keep quiet, to hide all feeling, to accept anything.

As we grew older, without our even noticing it, our muzzles grew tighter. Hide your pain in your heart, suffer in silence, unveiled pain only brings scandal and shame . . . Women were molded with these phrases and murmured them silently. I was one of those women, I still am.

Did my father – who publicly proclaimed to be the defender of honor and dignity, who had always protected the weaker and less privileged – think that his daughter had no need of paternal support? Or perhaps it was preferable to deal with the poor rather than his own grandchildren, a responsibility that would have been his if I deserted my husband, and to avoid scandal, to avoid losing face, dishonor. Let all stay hidden, everything tidy, and wash your hands of the whole business.

So after being taught to depend on men's support, to not defend yourself, we are dropped. At the moment we need help, we are left to fend with our fate. Our fate? Produce other males in their image and shut up? Were honor and dignity just words I had learned to mouth since my childhood? Were they empty words or words of men made for men alone?

Where could I go?

Where could I run with my children and pregnant up to my ears? Even if I had been able to put aside the respect I felt I owed my father, where could I go in 1945 in this country where small and great wars, locusts, epidemics, and famines came and went as they pleased without ever asking for an invitation.

Where could I go? Where does a nail without a head belong? I am ashamed, still ashamed. Even knowing today my only choice was death or resignation, I am ashamed down to the marrow of my bones and I will never forgive myself . . .

Every time Abdullah gets sick I think of that big glass ashtray, heavy as three plates, that hit Abdullah's skull, splitting open his forehead, an ashtray thrown by the man who revolts me so I can not call him my husband. Each time I think of the boot in my face, my lip opened, and I who do nothing. Each time my arm breaks again, my heart explodes, my body moans in pain and loathing because I do nothing. I did nothing to defend myself and nothing to defend my children. I let it happen, I've always just let things happen.

I am a coward. I am fearful and cowardly, a woman with no dignity, with no backbone. How can I accept that day when I could not muster up the strength to resist at all, not the slightest gesture? If only to spit in the face of these two men on their horses, even if the spit fell back in my face . . . At least I would have been able to tell myself, Dounia, you did what you could.

No.

I let myself be crushed by the pain, my tongue stuck to the roof of my mouth, my arms clutched at my sides. That's all. That's all I did. That's all I was capable of. When you give up once, it's over, you learn to give up for the rest of your life. The damage is done. You never struggle back on your feet. One resignation leads to another. Evil engenders evil. Endlessly.

I should have killed him, rid the world of his violence and madness, this man, this unworthy father of my children. I should have killed him with my bare hands to prevent our falling under his yoke, under his fists, under his boots . . .

The person my grandchildren love is not the woman buried under layers of fat, layers of sorrow and shame, but the child I was that returns to this body from time to time.

How can I tell my daughter that the sickness of her brother she so wishes me to explain to her is just a misfortune that befell him, when her father and all of his race should have been treated, when I, their mother, was the sick one? I am crazy to have loved a man who was crazy, to have had children with him, to have let him act uncontrollably, to have let him trample our whole family.

How can I admit to myself that my own lack of dignity destroyed my family, that my weakness and lack of courage pushed us over the edge. How can I admit to all the violence I accepted without ever reacting; how to speak of my shame, my resignation, my resentment, my bitterness, my cowardliness without wanting to die, without dying . . .

How can I tell the truth I've hidden so long, how can I say my father was a coward and a liar when I've always said he was a holy man. How can I say that deep in my heart I have no respect for him? How can I say I hate him without trembling?

How can I say I've lost all respect for my husband, the father of my children, that I have hated him at times, that what remains of my feelings for him is pity because he is old, lonely, and unhappy. I can't say that. He is their father after all. I've always taught my children to love and respect their father and I can not reveal all he has done and all that I haven't done.

It would be ridiculous to leave him now. I should have decided that long ago when my legs were still slim and my body strong, when I was wearing my wedding dress, before he tore it off . . . But I loved him . . . I still love him . . .

Today I wonder today who is more to blame. The person who strikes the blow, the person who lets themself be hit, or the person who watches and does nothing?

*Translated from the French by Jill McDougall*

# YOLANDE GEADAH

## VEILED WOMEN:
## UNVEILED FUNDAMENTALISM

*The Two Sides of the Coin*

It is quite natural to reflect on the meaning of the phenomenon of young Moslem girls living in the West deciding suddenly to wear the *hijab*, even though this practice is commonly associated with numerous restrictions imposed upon women. Is that a failure of integration, a re-awakening of religious zeal, or simply an assertion of identity? Is it the expression of Islamic activism or a response to parental coercion? Perhaps it is a little bit of each.

In Quebec as much as in France, the media and some researchers approached the issue of veiled young girls, questioning the latter on the reasons behind their decision. One must interpret the results of those investigations with some caution, lest one ends up blurring the issue instead of clarifying it. First, these studies explore only one side of the situation in that they deal with those who wear the veil out of personal conviction, since those who are forced into wearing it would not admit so publicly. In brief, even if the said studies contribute to a better understanding of the motives behind wearing the veil voluntarily, they fail to account for the phenomenon in its entirety.

## The Multiple Facets of the Veil

Many are puzzled by the account of those who advocate the veil. Some skeptics doubt the sincerity of these accounts and believe the young girls to be victims of brainwashing or of being themselves spokespersons for fundamentalist groups. Such a judgment shows a lack of understanding of the internal dynamics of the issue and the skillfulness of the fundamentalist movement which actively encourages women to wear the veil. It is necessary to recognize the fact that the latter would not have become so popular solely as the result of coercive measures and against the will of the women involved.

To be sure, on a personal level, the meaning of the veil varies with the people who wear it and the particular context in which they live. The personal reasons behind wearing the veil are often valid reasons in the eyes of those who opt for it, even if those reasons happen to be at the heart of religious doctrines advocating the veil. The concept of cognitive dissonance, a concept well-known in cognitive psychology, reveals quite well the reason for which people rationalize the motives of their behavior.

In the West, the religious discourse that advocates the veil is a rational discourse. Even though this discourse supports women's submissiveness and glorifies the patriarchal model based on male authority, it rather appeals to the intelligence and the loyalty of each believer. This discourse emphasizes the free choice of those who opt for the veil and exhorts liberal Moslems not to oppose the decision to wear it among their friends and relatives.

In order to adapt itself to the Western context, religious discourse will claim that wearing the veil should not hinder women from choosing any profession they would like to embrace. Paradoxically, however, it emphasizes also, in an increasingly formal manner, sexual segregation. For instance, those who opt for the veil are subsequently encouraged to avoid all contact with men outside their family; to refuse to sit next to or talk to a young man, let alone to touch his hand, and finally to befriend only veiled women. This discourse constantly deplores westernization and Women's liberation. It glorifies the assertion of Islamic identity, one based on the respect of traditions emphasizing sexual segregation.

We have to admit that the traditional model advocates certain advantages for veiled women even in a Western context. For instance, it speaks in favor of communal rather than individualistic values; it exhorts men to take full financial responsibility for the family, and it instills in youngsters a feeling of belonging and dignity. In some black disadvantaged districts in the United States, it seems that such religious discourse succeeded in steering young black Moslems away from drugs and other forms of delinquency while mobilizing them around Islamic causes, thus giving them a renewed sense of identity. Given these facts, it is not hard to comprehend the reasons behind the appeal and the liberating power of such discourse. The veil becomes the expression of a more conservative way of life, one at odds with Western value systems associated with the problems of modern society. As a result of this largely positive discourse, several women who opted for the veil do not see in their decision a gesture of hostility or constraint. The need for spirituality and the need to adopt various religious practices are not limited to Moslem women alone. Economic, social and political crises have made an increasing number of persons in Western countries take refuge in religion. The veil has been for many a way of exchanging the vicissitudes of modern life for the haven of peace promised by the traditional model.

In the case of France, the appeal of the fundamentalist movement promoting the veil has been profusely analyzed, namely in such books as François Gaspard and Farhad Khosrokhavan's *Le Voile et la république* published in Paris in 1995 (La Découverte). It was noted that this movement took birth in the exclusionary context of ghetto life, an exclusion further aggravated by unemployment and economic crises as well as violent anti-immigrant and anti-Islamic sentiments. All those conditions which go against integration may have caused some young Moslems born or having been raised in France, to lean towards fundamentalism, a movement which bestows on them a sense of dignity, while reaffirming their Moslem identity. In this light, wearing the veil acquires a dignifying way for some to assert an identity distinct from that of a majority to which they could never belong. This identity assertion takes place within a broader picture of a break-up with Western society, a society characterised by women's liberation and sexual permissiveness.

On the other hand, some young girls claim that wearing the veil allows for a more congenial family atmosphere by reassuring other members of the family about their good morality. In fact, it is common for immigrants in general (not only Moslems) to feel uneasy at the prospect of raising their children, especially girls, in a promiscuous social milieu. Hence, they impose upon their teenagers some restrictions that turn out to be even more rigid than the ones practiced in their country of origin, in order to limit their freedom of movement and thus reduce the risk of pre-marital sex. When the parental concern is expressed through pressure based on religious discourse, Moslem adolescent girls are more easily tempted to opt for the veil "voluntarily" in order to preserve peace at home. In such a case, wearing the veil takes the form of a strategy on their part, a concession allowing them to overcome the disadvantages of a restrictive family environment.

But what about girls who opt for the veil against the will of their liberal oriented parents? The most surprising justification for wearing the veil is probably given by some young girls who claim it gives them a sense of power and autonomy. No deception involved here. As an empowering device, the veil covers a host of realities. Some young girls assert that the veil gives them a new measure of freedom in their social relations by allowing them to assert themselves on an intellectual level rather than a physical one. Others explain that the veil provides them with a certain degree of independence in their interactions with their parents.

Strangely enough, the balance of power seems sometimes to be upturned in favor of those who adopt the veil despite the disagreement of their family. One witnesses a change of attitude in those girls: From shy and effaced, they suddenly become more assertive and self-confident, draped as they are in the virtue of the veil from which they draw a new legitimacy. They become so to speak "untouchable" in the eyes of their parents, especially so if the latter are opposed to fundamentalism. Parents take leave of their authority when faced with their daughter's determination to cover her head.

That seemingly incomprehensible situation is due to the fact that the power struggle between liberal and fundamentalist trends are played in favor of the latter. On a world scale, there is no question as to the political power of the fundamentalist movement which militantly advocates the veil. Groups and associations that encourage wearing the veil in the West are generally better organized, better financed and more militant than Moslems opposed to fundamentalism. Consequently, those who adopt the veil in spite of their more liberal milieu, change sides so to speak and go on the side of the stronger group.

Thus, young girls who insist on wearing the veil against their parents' will sometimes gain in prestige, autonomy and personal power. The commotion caused by the veil in the West as well as the movement which revolves around young veiled girls defending their individual right to wear it is an added incentive for them to maintain their stance. Finding themselves suddenly admired as heroines carrying the banner of Islam by those who value religious identity assertion, these young veiled girls acquire a new self-confidence and spontaneously project an assertive image which is extremely precious to the fundamentalist groups. They can become the best advocates of the veil among their girlfriends who are likely to emulate them out of solidarity, or in order to challenge their own parents and their society. In any case, their social status is thus enhanced through the veil.

These young girls are called on to play a leading role in proselytizing (daawa) campaigns of the fundamentalist movement. Adherence to such a movement constitutes the logical follow-up to the process of assertion of identity and personal growth. This membership allows them to further emancipate themselves from the narrow family milieu and to belong to a larger community which offers many benefits, including moral support. The appeal of a fundamentalist movement revolving around a community approach fills a large gap in the life of youngsters who otherwise dwell in the anonymity of large urban centers typical of a modern society.

Furthermore, the fundamentalist movement offers youngsters the possibility of marriage with a militant member of the group, a fact which is an actual improvement of the status of many of some Moslem girls. In this context, we can understand why the factor of voluntary self-marginalization derived from the fact of wearing the veil in a Western society can be easily outweighed by the overall advantages.

## The Strengths and Limitations of Personal Justifications

What personal justifications indicate first and foremost is that wearing the veil in the West beholds unsuspected advantages on a personal level. One is quick to notice that wearing the veil does not always carry a connotation of oppression for those women who opt for it, whether they do so out of religious conviction or as a survival strategy in a conservative milieu.

By asserting that wearing the veil is simply a symbol of identity assertion without expatiating on the resulting constraints for women, religious discourse advocating the veil has succeeded in convincing the most Westernized of Moslem women to adopt it. In fact, if it is true that the veil does not entail any professional, social or educational constraints, why then oppose it? It is precisely this ambiguity, deftly cultivated by fundamentalist discourse, that largely explains the success of the veil and the big appeal it has to Moslem women living in a Western society.

We have said that wearing the veil gives some the opportunity to assert their identity and by so doing, to challenge parental or institutional authority. In this light, claiming the veil by teenagers living in the West entails other types of anti-conformist behaviors. Strangely enough, it is the veil advocates in the West who claim somewhat arrogantly that "if society tolerates for young girls to dance topless in a bar, get drugged or follow the punk fashion, why would it not tolerate them wearing the veil?" The argument rallies many proponents of the freedom of expression in support of the veil.

This superficial comparison ignores the fact that most school regulations forbid drugs or unusual clothes. The confusion is hereby maintained between that which is tolerated by society as a whole in the name of individual freedom, and that which is tolerated within school boundaries and the educational system. Based on the same logic, school regulations which forbid marginalization through clothes should also forbid the wearing of the veil, an argument which is refuted by those very same people who then claim the veil as a religious symbol.

Another type of argument opposes the ill effects of promiscuous behavior to the beneficial effects of conservatism associated with the veil. Why accept the fact that adolescents dress in a sexually provocative way, engage in precocious sex and become pregnant, and yet, on the other hand, oppose those who want to wear the veil and keep away from guys? This form of moral justification is very convincing, not only to Moslems. I believe it was precisely around this argument that a network of inter-ethnic solidarity was woven. Those who are nostalgic of more traditional interaction between the sexes are more numerous than one may think; they belong to a variety of cultures and religions.

This argument points in the direction of a certain uneasiness due to rapid changes in traditions, towards sexual

permissiveness among adolescents. The social problems resulting from those changes (emotional disturbance, teenage
pregnancies, school dropouts) seem more frequent in modern societies no longer subject to rigid religious norms.
Secular society seems not to have succeeded in establishing
new guidelines in this area. Fear of sexually transmitted
diseases remains for many the only valid yet insufficient
drive to solve the problem. Consequently, the return to
traditional religious values may appear to many as the only
safe ground.

*Emancipation Under the Veil*

One remains shaken by the claim put forward by some
young girls that wearing the veil has, so to speak, set them
free in their interaction with boys who no longer regard
them as objects but as human beings. The veil would thereby
mean for those girls a refusal to validate their identity by
physical attributes, a fact currently overrated in Western
culture. In fact, from a feminist point of view, considering all
the films and magazines where women's bodies are exploited, all the sex shops and provocative advertisements
seen in the subway, etc., wouldn't one wish sometimes to
hide one's own body and head with a veil so as to escape
from this overgeneralized sexual exploitation?

It is possible indeed to establish a parallel between the
argument in favor of the veil and the principle guiding the
choice of many Western women who prefer to dress soberly
in order to gain respectability. For instance, professional
women know for a fact that provocative clothes, especially
on the work site, encourage another type of interaction,
often to women's disadvantage. Women's sexual power is
often exploited to the advantage of men. Ironically, seen in

this light, the veil would thus be an antidote to the sexism associated with modern life; a sort of "emancipation" for women who refuse to be considered as mere sexual objects. If such arguments were to be taken at face value, feminists all over the world should hasten to wear the veil!

All things considered, why is it not possible to transform a symbol of oppression into a symbol of emancipation and assertion? *A priori*, nothing prevents the belief that it is possible to put an old outfit to a new use. For all its appeal, this logic hides a gross mystification. Unfortunately, it does not incumb on a few, no matter how sincere they are, to bestow on the veil a sense of emancipation while at the same time it is being actively advocated by a powerful fundamentalist movement that is openly in favor of inequality of the sexes and that strives to limit women's participation to the sole domestic sphere.

Various strategies are used by the fundamentalist movement to paint a more cheerful picture or else to understate the constraints pertaining to women, claiming various necessary exceptions in order to serve its cause. This fact does not change the social model which upholds the veil. The negative connotations associated to the veil are too important to allow Moslem women to reject them in totum, the more so since there does not exist a movement claiming to transform the veil into a symbol of a social vision geared towards egalitarian and democratic principles.

## Poisoned Compromises

The situation with Iranian women is instructive in many aspects even though it belongs to an altogether different context. One still recalls the pictures shown by the media in 1978, featuring militant Moslem women demonstrating on the streets of Teheran and wearing voluntarily the veil *(Tchador)* as a symbol of their liberation from the Western model imposed by the Shah. Hopes elicited by the Islamic revolution were still boundless. Some Iranian women rallied in favor of the Ayatollah regime and acted as a police force to impose the Tchador on all women. The more eloquent amongst them have condemned the intrusion of Western feminists who exhibited solidarity with Iranian feminists resisting the Tchador.

In retrospect, we can in fact admit the strategical error of Western feminists who were tangled in this sad incident. As in Egypt at the beginning of the Century, accusations of Western intrusions acted as efficient means of intimidation allowing to discredit internal opposition and to erect a barrier between Moslem women and other women. Those accusations succeeded in eroding the efforts of international solidarity which otherwise would have been threatening to the patriarchal power. This missed historical rendez-vous has disappointed many progressive Westerners who, today, no longer dare speak against the veil for fear of being accused of racism or cultural colonialism.

However desirable it may be to expose the strategical error of Western feminists, one has rarely ventured to ana-lyze in full the strategy used by progressive Iranian women and Moslem forces who have supported the Ayatollah's regime. As soon as it gained power, the new theocratic regime went ahead and destroyed all the democratic compo-nents of the country, including those which had given it their "strategic" support. One can draw many lessons from such poisoned alliances and compromises meant to be temporary but which eventually led to obvious regressions on the level of basic freedoms.

On the other hand, it is true that within the Ayatollah's regime, men and women managed after all to bypass the oppressive regime of the Tchador and to forge themselves some spaces of freedom. This fact suffices to relieve the conscience of pragmatically inclined souls who will assert that one should not therefore blow out of proportion the disadvantages related to the veil and to religious totalitarianism. This cynicism comes from a reductive vision where the trees hide the forest. Many well-intentioned individuals would thus be misled.

Once more, the real danger does not really come from girls who adopt the veil, but from the fact that the veil is part and parcel of a totalitarian system and ideology that tend to deny basic freedoms. If it is true that a certain number of women succeed in escaping from the restrictive implications of the veil. This, however, does not apply to the majority of Moslem women. We should distinguish between the practical, immediate and individual interest of some women, from the strategic and collective interest of the majority of Moslem women, on a long term basis. I believe it possible to escape on an individual level from the significant restrictions imposed by a repressive system, whether with or without the veil. In the current context, however, everything seems to point out the fact that, no matter how inoffensive the veil may seem, sooner or later it becomes a heavy trap which stifles the most legitimate aspirations of those who opt for it. There is no doubt that the Islamic and Western contexts are very different from one another and that the consequences of wearing the veil will thus be different in each of these contexts. However, even if women who wear the veil in the West experience this as a dignifying gesture, it still holds true that one day they will have to submit to religious laws which deny the equality of the sexes and certain fundamental rights. In France, some Imams publicly assert the primacy of Islamic teachings over those of the state, and the primacy of Islamic law over French secular law.

## A False Protection

The idea that a woman can be set free by wearing a veil that protects her from male's looks is at best a temporary illusion. Wearing a veil in the West attracts people's attention and does not in the least atone for men's libido, to judge from the attitude of those who actively advocate the veil. In societies where the veil has been the norm, men look at women in as concupiscent and bold a way as can be.

Even when covered from head to foot women are closely eyed the moment they appear in public. They are often attacked by males overstimulated by the sight of a hair lock or an uncovered ankle. This is a universal human reality that transcends all cultures. It would seem that the more rigorous and puritanical societal norms are, the more aggressive male sexual behavior becomes. Worthy of note is that most religions claim to honor women by imposing a division between the sexes, all the while bestowing a superiority on the male, a fact which instills in boys and men the despise of women.

The so-called glorification of a veiled woman as opposed to the degradation of the woman-object of modern culture is a myth. The popularity, amongst veiled women, of lewd underwear deemed degrading by many non-veiled women, is in fact surprising. It seems that in the present context, especially the Western one, wearing the veil carries as a function, not to "liberate" women from men's sexual harassment, as some will claim, but rather to "confiscate" their power of attraction in favor of men in their own family.

The opposition between the exploitation of women's bodies in a liberal system and the merit behind wearing the veil in a traditional society rests on a shaky reasoning: The virtues of a patriarchal system are compared to the vices and excesses of more liberal a system. For the sake of honesty, such a comparison should be based on the pros and cons of each of these systems. One would thus notice that the protection afforded women in a traditional system is largely tarnished by a number of restrictions and abuses that hinder the realisation of their potential in all domains. The protective aspect is soon transformed into an unbearable tyranny for those males and females who are subjected to it. A comparative study would probably reveal that incest, rape, prostitution and all sorts of abuses are as frequent, if not more so, in traditional societies as in modern Western societies.

What is the value of respectability and the protection bestowed on women, without the recognition of their full rights and freedom? Is the "protection" bestowed by a male in a patriarchal system preferable to that which can be offered by a democratic, secular and rightful society? Those women who pass for being "protected" in a traditional family system are treated as second-class citizens and their most elementary human rights are often denied. One could compare nostalgic advocates of the inequality of the sexes to those individual in bygone times who used to be against the abolition of slavery. After all, liberated slaves were suddenly subjected to the harsh conditions of the proletariat, whereas before, they could be luckily under the protection of a just and generous master. Alas, freedom carries with it costs and risks that constitute the very essence of human condition.

## The Gentle Face of Fundamentalism

By revealing a truth that often escapes us, the testimonial of Moslem young girls advocating the veil at school has that advantage of breaking up certain stereotypes of which we are often unaware.

We will have probably noticed that in Quebec as much as in France, most of those girls who advocate the veil were often born and raised in the West and thus, they were never subjected to the constraints linked to fundamentalist ideology. It often happens, for instance, that Western women converted to Islam through marriage become more adamant about wearing the veil than Moslem-born women. Some of those women exhibit exemplary zeal in proselytizing. Thus, a French-Canadian woman (Fabienne L'Escadre) converted to Islam is President of the Association of Moslem Women in Quebec (*La Presse,* February 2, 1992).

Likewise, in France, some associations of Moslem women, such as the one belonging to the Isère Department, are directed by French women converted to Islam. Their experience of Western networks is a precious asset in swaying public opinion in favor of the veil and other religious doctrines. The defense and advocacy of the veil in the West are part of an organised network including associations, support committees, press releases, hunger strikes, official protests, etc. In Quebec, the case which opened the door to the polemic about the veil in September 1994 was not linked to immigration. The teenager involved had been born catholic and later converted to Islam. Everything seems to indicate that young women, especially teenagers who insist the most on wearing the veil in the West, are often unaware of all the social and political stakes attached to it.

This is not an "insult" to women who adopt the veil out

of religious conviction, nor is it an infantilization of them. History has proven that every social and political system, no matter how repressive it is, gets established and proliferates thanks to the collaboration and support, whether voluntary or not, of those who manage to benefit from it. We have seen that the veil brings advantages to its advocates, whether active or not. No need thereby to doubt the sincerity, the intelligence or the justifications of the proponents of the veil. However, their testimonial cannot replace analysis nor dictate people's position vis-à-vis the question.

Could we believe, as some assert, that we are concerned in the West by one facet only of the question, namely the right of those who advocate the veil? Of course we cannot deny the existence of a serious difference between the imposed veil in Islamic societies and the chosen veil in the West. These two dimensions belong to a different step in the process of expansion of the fundamentalist movement which seeks today to spread its influence wherever there is a Moslem community. However, judging from the internal dynamic of the veil, nothing justifies the optimism of those who think that we are affected in the West by only one dimension of this reality. In fact, if we are to consider the progressive evolution of the phenomenon, the two dimensions seem inseparable in time and space. As we have seen, Islamic proselytism begins by a persuasion campaign destined to win as many believers as possible to the veil, then it becomes more and more invading and threatening to those who refuse to conform.

This explains the panic of Algerian women living in France or in Quebec, who are well aware of this internal dynamic. They are worried that the fact of allowing the veil in public schools in order to satisfy the demands of some would lead to its propagation in their community, a fact which would expose them to harassment and growing pressures to yield to that practice.

And yet some intellectuals continue to believe that the religious proselytism now quite visible within Moslem communities living in the West has nothing to do with the political fundamentalism which causes upheavals in Moslem societies. The distinction between "extreme" and "moderate" fundamentalism, as well as the converging of social and political fundamentalism, are very helpful in order to point out the dangers hidden behind soft fundamentalism.

In the 1980s, in many cities in France, Canada, the U.S., and elsewhere, an Islamic activism of a nature altogether different from what existed before suddenly took birth. Gilles Kepel, in his 1994 book entitled *À l'ouest d'Allah* (Seuil) has portrayed the results of his large study on Islam in the West, showing clearly that Moslems living in the West are called upon to build a community asserting its own specificity. Islamic associations endowed with a social and religious mission have flourished in various regions of France, in view of a better organization of their political activities; they are grouped under the auspices of Union des Organisations Islamiques en France (UOIF) (Union of Islamic Organizations in France). According to *L'Express,* (November 17, 1994), the Association Educative des Musulmans (Educational Association of Moslems) recruits its members amongst Moslem delinquents which it sets on the right path. It advocates wearing the veil at school and supports the campaign against school authorities. Some Islamic activists mentor school groups for problem students, a fact which also allows them to propagate a social vision inspired by fundamentalist philosophy. It is precisely this politico-religious activism which largely explains the appearance of the veil in the West. It is obvious that what is aimed at is the revival of religious fervor amongst members of Moslem communities living in exile, in order to enlist their inside help to the fundamentalist movement.

In North America, the phenomenon of the veil and the Islamic mobilisation seem less pronounced than in France. This mobilisation, however, will follow a similar trajectory insofar as the economic destructuralization which causes exclusion will facilitate its task. In the United States, where racial discrimination has been for a long time a source of economic exclusion and of serious tensions, Islamic activism is flourishing. It has chosen to rely mainly on black communities. Louis Farrakhan, a charismatic leader of a black Islamic movement, seeks to put the demands of Black Americans under the banner of Islam. In that way, the network of the Moslem fundamentalist movement continues to spread according to a decentralized mode which lessens its internal cohesion but enlarges its popular base. Strangely, it seems that it seeks to compensate for the saturation point it has reached in Islamic societies by the enthusiasm of its new members in Western societies.

Sometimes funded from the outside, but often supported by an internal volunteer base, this social and religious activism fits into a system with wider political goals. It gives its partisans a certain prestige and gratifies them, if not with some economic advantages, at least with a feeling of power originating in the leading role played within the community, in the service of a sacred cause. For the moment, this religious militancy which actively advocates the veil and other practices more and more restrictive to women, offers a gentle and respectable face, a fact which allows it to act as it pleases, since it does not violate established rules.

In fact, I believe that the religious activism proliferating at the moment in Quebec and in Canada is not always directly linked to political fundamentalism. Some of its most fervent advocates seem sincerely opposed to the fundamentalist movements which have torn apart Islamic societies. The problem stems from the fact that this activism which aims at reviving religious fervor in its members through the observance of rigid religious principles, may lead the way to the spread of a politico-religious activism which may soon emerge.

Women who opt for the veil are sometimes very active advocates of a fundamentalist vision of society, and sometimes passive members who adopt practices advocated by the fundamentalist movement without necessarily agreeing with the goals of the latter, or without fully appreciating their consequences. Therefore, it would be more accurate to speak of different levels of awareness among various members of the movement. Thus, veiled women become political instruments; they contribute in one way or another to the pursuit of the goals of the fundamentalist movement. In the present context, accepting to wear the veil is to give an added ammunition to those who try to promote a system in which the religious governs the political.

Finally, while the fundamentalist vision infiltrates the collective conscience, and the movement gains in power and influence, supported by active members of its community, it increasingly denies basic rights and the principles of equality of all citizens.

*Translated from the French by Elizabeth Dahab*

N.B. For the purpose of clarity, the word *hijab* or veil here refers to a scarf that covers the hair and the ears It is not to be confused with the full veil covering the face and the body, as in Saudi Arabia, nor with the *Tchador* in Iran (Translator's remark).

# NADIA GHALEM

## BLUE NIGHT

## *Turbulences*

The airplane gained altitude while falling through the holes in the air. They announced turbulence. Some of the passengers were perspiring profusely. Over there, in the front, a child was crying. Everyone was breathing to the rhythm of the swaying of the huge 747.

Alya was reveling in it. As a little girl, she had been crazy about swings, elevators, slides, and everything that made her stomach leap by going a little bit higher, a little bit faster, a little bit wilder. She loved to feel that her body was light, free, almost non-existent. It gave her the impression that her flesh had dissolved to give place to the emotions and the soul . . . Had she embarked on all these journeys just for this, for turbulence? Nothing had forced her to leave her spotless apartment, nestled on the slopes of Mont-Royal, to take interminable naps in scorching heat in a noisy boarding house in Rome's piazza de Espagne.

Nothing? A streak of lightning flashed across her imagination – a streak of lightning like that deadly look from the man who she was trying to find again from beyond the continents and the oceans. She hardly knew him, but from the day that their paths crossed in the midst of a noisy crowd, her life had changed; they were engaged in a huge chess

match of looks, love letters, and hateful indifference, like
Kleist's tragic heroes who call out to one another to break
each other's hearts. Starting with a barely hinted smile,
passion swooped down on them, like the eagle on his prey,
above all on her, who was at once vulnerable, fragile, and
gasping for breath like prey; but also cruel, relentless, and
wild like the eagle.

Alya could hardly remember what her life had been like
before this turbulence. It was like a distant dream. Her days
had been split between the office and the apartment. She
busied herself with the stories and dramas of others. She had
chosen the career of a lawyer, almost unconsciously, because
she wanted to share the good fortune that had given her a
carefree childhood and an economically secure existence.
Did she feel guilty for the life that had sheltered her from the
poverty, divorce, financial worries, and heartache that made
so many other women shudder and weep? Alya Nabralovna
the lawyer was all the more able to overcome these problems
in that she was perfectly estranged from them; she had the
power to approach her clients' sorrows rationally and logi-
cally. Sometimes men consulted her as well; it made no
difference to her. They all became rather like children that
she had to defend and counsel in complete equity. In this
way, she became known as one of the city's best lawyers.
After her studies, money had come without too much effort.
This did not prevent her imagination from roaming far and
wide. Alya Nabralovna, Esq. dreamed of travel, but not to
Caribbean beaches where she would have to get a tan to
show her colleagues that she had the means to shorten the
overly-long Montreal winter, and that she was successful
enough to be able to afford a little off-season get-away. Of
course, she supported all the campaigns against world hun-

ger, for the safety of children in war-torn countries, etc.; in short, she was socially involved all the more gladly because her engagements did not invite criticism and suffered from no ambiguity as far as political opinions were concerned. Why then did her life seem so comfortably boring? She had given herself all the adventures that a forty-year-old woman, financially independent and emotionally unattached, could give herself. Sometimes she remembered, not without tenderness, the man who had loved her regardless of all social conventions and who she had so cruelly cast aside. At the time, his suffering had tremendously irritated her. He ended up considering her a "monstrously egotistical being." She had laughed. She had not understood how someone could be so melodramatic about a missed adventure. Her clients' cases seemed less real, less near; she took them more seriously.

Sometimes she caught herself envying the grand heartbreaks of others, but Alya Nabralovna was strong enough to not lose face. Just to see, out of curiosity, she would have liked to experience love, that superhuman sentiment that seemed to crush its victims under an overwhelming weight. It was summer and the radios of all the world's capitals resonated with Carmen's refrain: "Si tu ne m'aimes pas, je t'aime, et si je t'aime, prends garde à toi!"

"Prends garde à toi!" sounded like a warning shot, a declaration of war, an explosion. The worst was becoming beautiful. It is this strange beauty that Nabralovna, Esq. wanted to know, and that she simultaneously feared. She sometimes said to herself, with a touch of despair, that great loves, like accidents, only happened to others, and without doubt she was a member of that category of people who cross the plane of existence more as spectators than as actors.

She felt the same fervor, the same desire, the same communion in the presence of her distraught clients that the critic feels before the artist and his artwork. Until now, Alya had experienced nothing except the polite exchanges, cloaked in the experience of daily life, that lead to marriage or romance; but never had she known this giddiness made of questions and answers, of advances and retreats, this giddiness that weaves, with its failures and successes, the most wonderful, the most violent, and the most haunting of dialogues between two people.

Why had she decided one night, after an exhausting office meeting, to attend the dedication dinner for the third congress of the Bar?

The apartment seemed frigid to her after the heated discussions in the smoky, noisy atmosphere. She hardly took the time to shower and change her clothes, without giving much attention to what her colleagues called "the look," the new way that the new conquerors of the labor market and business dressed themselves, the suit of the fighters who remind one of the feminists of the American magazines. She was waiting for someone to notice her for something other than her hairstyle or the quality of her blouses. However, that night, he whom she privately called "the man from somewhere else" did not notice her. When then? The next day? She vaguely remembered a coldly-lit room. Those present had to put up with the tiring boasts of a speaker more concerned with concealing his knowledge than with revealing it. Then, like children who become accomplices in amusing themselves at the expense of a boring teacher, she and the man seated next to her cracked jokes; they competed with each other in making witty comments and disrespectful remarks. When the speaker stepped down, she saw a stranger heading her way, his face lit by a smile, a twinkle in his blue eyes, as if he had always known her. He asked her what her specialty was; she answered: "matrimonial law." The word divorce horrified her. His was union law; he did not use the word "political."

Alya Nabralovna had thoroughly combed through her memory, but she no longer remembered the two or three sentences that they had spoken next. Had she unwittingly appeared provocative? Had he decided, from the peak of his Mediterranean arrogance, to break the ice of this woman who dared to answer him without losing her composure? They exchanged business cards.

He left for his own country and she for her office and her apartment until the day when she received a perfectly formal letter informing her that he would be in such-and-such a place on such-and-such a date, one of those meetings where specialists spouting esoteric jargon flaunt the knowledge they spent so many years in acquiring. She would have been able to ignore the message. She spent two long days composing a handwritten card in a neutral and distant style.

Doubt tortured her. She no longer knew if she had imagined the especially warm attitude that the stranger had adopted with her and if there was really any sentiment at all on his side. From watching her clients' situations, she knew that the men of certain cultures are more willing to display emotions that they afterwards forget all too quickly. She began to think about him in a more precise fashion. What kind of life did he lead? Was he married? Did he have children? She tried to imagine him. She had forgotten the exact form of his face; she was imbibed with the colour of his eyes and the strange sensation that his brief presence had awakened in her. As a result, Alya Nabralovna steadily slipped towards a new lifestyle, a new world view. She lived in the shadow of a man who was on the other side of the world, more completely than if he had been there, nearby; time and distance rendered him more living, more real than if he had been physically present. Now he had a place in her personal universe, on the same level as her parents or childhood friends. She could not imagine her life without him. Distant and absent, he was only more haunting.

She traveled to the convention in Paris. It was there that things began to get complicated. He looked at her with a sort of intimacy, but he remained aloof through his words and gestures. She said to herself, "Our thoughts outpace our capacity to advance." For the first time in her life, a man frightened her. Did he fear her as well? Perhaps they had the foreboding that the hurricane of their sentiments would wreck havoc on their respective and well-organized lives.

The torment of love and the confusion of uneasy sadness could not be allowed to invade coldly rational professional activities. That would be revolution, anarchy. She had to resist. She resisted by trying to convince herself that he had been making fun of her, that he had manipulated her, that he was neither as naive nor as vulnerable as he seemed. He had provoked a situation that he had allowed to drag on at his pleasure without ever openly declaring his intentions or completely withdrawing. It was cruel. Alya Nabralovna loved even this cruelty.

The haunting question always returned: how did she get here, to this endless battle? To this all-encompassing dream? To this life wrapped up in iron fetters spanning distance and time to link two hearts? From one airport to another, from one telephone call to another, two people sought each other like the sun that rends the clouds of dawn to rejoin the horizon where it will sink at the end of the day, like the sea that covers the beach and retreats with a sigh. From his place on the other side of the world, did the man pretend to have forgotten? Alya sent a single word: silence. In her turn, she strove to think of something else, then an ambiguous invitation reached her. She packed her bags and rushed over, only to collide with the absence of someone who always had last minute missions.

Meanwhile, Spain's Square in Rome resonated with the mournful echoes of the poetry of Byron and Shelley, and the questions returned like torture: what compelled her, Alya Nabralovna, to ceaselessly take the same airplanes, to constantly invent excuses to return to the city where he, a mysterious shadow, lived? As if the distance was not enough, he still had to hide behind his absences, whether or not they were deliberate. A friend who took pride in psychology had said to her, "One never loves by chance." Why was she madly in love with a man she would most likely never see again?

"Do you like chess?" a gray-haired official had asked her. The incriminating question pierced straight to her heart. The game of chess, he clarified. She had not responded. She saw herself clearly, running from a black square to a white square, crossing zones of shadow and light, nights, days, a commonplace little pawn who would go and collapse at the feet of a rook or a royal piece of marble wielded by invisible hands in order to achieve the triumphant: checkmate! Who would dare to confront the king? He who, from the height of his arrogant chauvinism, was so skilled at alternating seductive, tender glances with the most injurious expressions of mockery.

Alya Nabralovna wanted to die. She felt simultaneously

manipulated and manipulating. She was an accomplice to a situation that would ruin her. She was tired of walking the streets of the city, of running from one fountain to another, those landmarks of stone and water, which seemed pregnant with symbolism to her, like so many refreshing oases bursting forth in the heart of sun-crushed city squares. Then she entertained fond memories of long snowy trails running under the trees across the Quebecan forest. She heard the whisper of skis on ice and saw the frost sparkling between her glance and the sky. A black horseman emerged from the powdery, white tempest; in his hand he had a mirror that reflected the sun. The alternation between light and shadow brought her back to the marble chessboard on which she had been competing since her entrance into the world, a small piece, hard but fragile, slipping perilously in the network of powers and provoking, eliciting by her movements, unforeseen relations between dark or light pawns. During the night, the fountains murmured loving whispers; during the day they echoed with the blaring of horns and the noise of the city.

"Say to the beloved that there is no terror save that of his absence." An unknown prisoner had written these words in the color of blood on the walls of Saint-Ange castle; there Stendhal had dreamed of the abbess of Castro and of Vanina Vanini's betrayal. The old stones continued to reflect the names of the lovers who had disappeared there. "Si je t'aime, prends garde-toi." Perhaps she had let her guard down. Perhaps she preferred this suffering of unhappy love over her old peaceful happiness?

Far off, in the Montreal tranquillity, a spotless apartment had sheltered the uneventful days of Alya Nabralovna, Esq., and the gray stone facades had been mute. The summers jostled one another to give way to the endless season of ice and cold. One could wait there for one's destiny or rush forward and burn one's wings, like the light-enchanted butterfly that flies into the flame and is burnt. Henceforth there would be a succession of missed dates and half-silences . . . Like the addict loves his drugs, like the child-martyr loves its executioner parents, Alya loved even the absence of a man who existed only in her dreams. She had deliberately prolonged this last trip; she did not want to leave the city and more. Sometimes she could see herself, several years in the future, like the old beggar who haunted the fountains of Rome raving about her lost loves and laughing in isolation. "You should go back home," her Roman friend told her, "you're going to make yourself mad!" She had laughed heartily. Me, mad?, come on. Alya Nabralovna had never felt like this: so alive, such a part of the world; she was glowing. Then the beautiful Roman woman added, absent-mindedly smoothing her gray hair, "He must love you too, but sometimes men lack courage in situations like this." Perhaps it was the word "courage" that had caused a kind of internal explosion, an implosion in Alya's mind and heart; from that moment on, she felt beautiful and broken, like a crystal garden.

Now Nabralovna, Esq. would return to Montreal under the conviction that she would never again see the face that had so disrupted her life, that she would never again hear that voice with the lilting accent. Never again? She would not be able to survive on such a conviction; she had to imagine that she would meet his alternately humble, domineering, choleric, childish, or astonished gaze again and again and say to herself that this was the man of her destiny, he who had thrown himself into the surface of her peaceful life like a rock and was still making waves.

In Rome, she spent entire days wandering through the grass and dust of imperial forums, daydreaming of the glories and defeats, the hatreds and loves that were exchanged there. Only broken marble pillars gave silent witness to the fragile human silhouettes that had haunted these places over the centuries, the sculptures, the graffiti, like the shadows on the wall after the explosion in Hiroshima. Now there was nothing left, nothing but words, names, phrases, and poems etched on these walls from time immemorial, written on the stone by hands that were now gone. Thus she, Alya Nabralovna, had walked among the ruins while persuading herself that she carried within her an undying love for a man who would perhaps never know it. In this state she had gone back and forth between Rome and Montreal, convinced that she was living the most formidable and painful of joys. In the airplane, the flight attendant was eyeing her strangely. They were going to land at Mirabel soon.

Turbulence . . . She had not told anyone she was coming, but she secretly hoped that someone would come to meet her, with a nice, warm coat, him, perhaps, with his mocking and vaguely protective smile. She shivered . . . Her Roman friend had told her, "You think that the poets and the novelists are making it up, and then one day . . . you love so deeply that you can no longer think of anything else. I was lucky; I got up one morning and said to myself, 'It's over.' Since then I have managed to live somehow, but before, I followed him to the ends of the earth." Alya heard herself respond, "I don't want this to end," and she gazed intensely at the sad and serene face of the beautiful Roman woman.

Do the airplanes that streak across the sky know that sometimes they carry clandestine loves? The Canadian customs official is convinced that Alya Nabralovna does not need to declare what she is bringing back into the country. Her bags are full of papers covered with feverish graffiti stolen from the walls of Rome, but her face has the serenity of the martyrs and the saints. The blank-expressioned official lets her pass.

Yes, someone is waiting over there, behind the window, with a coat slung over his arm; he is smiling. It does not really matter if it is not the great Roman love. Alya Nabralovna feels very tired. They help her into a taxi that will soon stop before a huge Victorian building. They ask Alya for her name and address. They take her to a beautiful, spotless bed. She stretches out on it with a sigh of relief. She hopes they will give her medication that will make her sleep for a long time.

A man in gray with tortoise shell glasses says to her, "I am Doctor Robitaille, your psychiatrist." She smiles faintly and responds, "I am Alya Nabralovna; I hear the music of the Roman fountains . . . I just got off an airplane where there was a lot of turbulence . . ."

*Translated from the French by Sharon Hathaway*

# MONA LATIF GHATTAS

## THE DOUBLE TALE OF EXILE

They loved each other until the thawing of the snows, until the melting of the finest film of ice on the roads. They saw the eruption of the buds of spring and the magnificent green of the maple trees in summer. He loved this country as one loves the woman who rears one. Completely. He learned her language and bequeathed to her fragments of his own. He had come from so far away, from a world so old that its phonemes echoed like the oracles that haunt our ever-changing imaginations. She had taken him into her home without the least prejudice, without even asking him the origin of his name. Amazed by the beauty of his mahogany skin and the profound gaze of the black eyes that pierced his silence, she patiently repeated words that he did not understand. He listened attentively to them, with the ardent desire of including them in his destiny.

With the shyness of the brave who have survived the wounds of History and in the praise-worthy innocence of those who will never know by what miracle they have weathered the passage of time, they unconsciously exchanged the codes of their knowledge. She opened all the skylights of his mind for him. He never wearied of admiring her, her and this country, her and the changing, cyclical landscape from which he learned that everything is reborn by the force of life. Between them were woven slender threads, stubborn threads that only appeared to give way in the face of History's blackmail, tangled lianas where migratory birds rest in the warmth of memory.

Having allowed him to enter her closed habitation, from which she traveled only in dreams, she unconsciously and simultaneously opened the doors of the universe. Grandmother of a continent of snow where several layers of History had already muffled the truth, fascinated by the troubling mystery of this rebellious descendant fleeing from the mad fire of an Anatolian desert on the edge of the Orient and Occident, she allowed his traces of foreignness make their mark on her: his snatches of memory and his staggering, fantastic tale of one night of life, one day of terror, one infinitesimal second of extreme lucidity. Once more she discovered that sorrow never dies, that it lives one hundred years, and perhaps one thousand, that forgetfulness does not exist, and that only a welcoming embrace, both familiar and foreign, miraculously succeeds in cauterizing the living evil.

Later, she will try to tell him that the most profound depths of this work were given to him by nature of his beauty – he who knew how to exhume that which had hidden under the weight of silence in the wounded depths of her soul – but he will be gone, and she will call out to him. She will immortalize him by calling out to him, recounting his journey in order that his memory may haunt the night of those who did not know how to discern between truth and falsity.

She will immortalize him while calling out to him, while waiting for the season to change.


Her name is Madeleine.

Long ago, her name was Manitakawa. That was during

a now distant childhood, thanks to the passing of time. The wise rejoice at its passage. The foolish complain.

For a long time now she had been Manitakawa alias Madeleine. When she still had red skin and hair so dark that it melted into the night, her mother kept a tavern to support the family. Each day, after returning from school, she would put down her bag, put on an apron, and start to wash the beer mugs stacked up in the sink. Often boorish drunks in search of a diversion would call her, laughing while they deformed her name. Wanawana . . . come here . . . Ninikaka . . . Takataka . . . In the back alcove she would shed tears of anger which would fall in the soapsuds and disappear down the drain.

When she was twelve, she declared loudly that her name was Madeleine. She hardly had the time to announce her new name when a voice more bawdy than the others followed her drooling into the back alcove. At present, a veil concealed what followed, but it was at this moment that her features hardened into the ugliness that terror can inscribe on a face.

Madeleine was seized so violently that she swallowed a cry that wedged itself in her throat. Suddenly her voice became rough. The small seed of beauty under her nostril hardened, and slowly her body began to thicken, as if it wanted to become forever a wall, a watchtower, or a castle keep.

Madeleine had the impression that she had become ugly. She no longer looked at herself in the mirror, and since men only cast eyes at the beautiful and women take great pains not to stare at ugliness for fear that it will rub off on them, Madeleine found herself, like all of humanity's rebels, isolated from the world.

Long years had passed.

Since then, her skin had paled strangely and threads of silver mingled with the black of her bun. At present she lived in the heart of a large city, mixing with people who never spoke to her, drowning in the noise of the seven machines of the laundry room where she worked in the fourth basement of the large hospital on White Cedars Avenue. Dressed in a large smock, she invariably bustled around from seven to three, an astonishing lightness in her movements and an astonishing stability in her person. The white smock gave her the appearance of a well-established snowbank between the faded green walls.

Robust and secretive, Madeleine held a rare job for a woman. She was a launderer. In laundry rooms, woman are usually assigned to the sorting, to the drying room, to the radiator grill, to counting, or to the autoclave. It is always a man who assumes the position of launderer. Attaching the huge sacks to the mouth of the washing machine and loading five hundred pounds of laundry at a time demands a special strength. One day, by popular vote, Madeleine, who had previously been "manager of the radiator grill," replaced the launderer who had just injured his back under the weight of a sack of laundry. As he was never able to return to work, she kept this job which seemed to give her profound satisfaction and which she performed with great dexterity.

Surrounded by the humidity and the smell of bleach, Madeleine worked in silent cheerfulness. She almost never spoke. She only responded when someone asked her a question. She directed her eyes where necessary for her work, but she never looked at other people. She worked with a cheerfulness that revealed itself so clearly through her gestures and movements that no one could miss it.

If someone asked her why she felt so at ease in this place, she would have responded that the noise of the dryer, the spin-dryer, and the radiator grill resembled the sound of trains coming into a station, giving her the perpetual illusion of returning from a trip. Of course, worktime being consecrated to making a living and saving for a vacation, no one asked her this type of question.

Thus, for several long years, depending on the time of day, Madeleine loaded the washing machine with the sheets that they called "rags" from the white sacks, the contaminated laundry from the red sacks that meant "danger," and the laundry from the green sacks that they sterilized for the surgical unit. First she did the alkali pre-rinse, then the two washing cycles with a powerful detergent, then she carefully measured the finishing powder.

*Translated from the French by Sharon Hathaway*

# NADINE LATIF

## THE METAMORPHOSES OF ISHTAR

### III

May Allah deliver us from the son of Adam, said my
    governess
From the man of war and rage
may God spare you O Montreal
from what my eyes have seen
those eyes that eternally stare endlessly
since 1975
since my first EXILE

### IV

I was leaving to Cairo
To the Nile misery
To the empty stomachs
And eyes that feed on dust.
Straight to the cradle of hunger ma Dame,
I should have known
That the cradle was in me
That the cradle was me,
and that the people of Egypt was I.
I was hungry.
But my hunger refused food.
I refused to see the alleys and ghettos of Cairo
Refused to see those thin hungry masses.

## V

I rush to you
O Montreal
Winter,
Winter that leaves me no mercy.
I have seen the graves of blood on your frozen land
for fire does not melt
but iron surrounds your body
and iron does not melt
Winter-Age of steel –
you resemble the harshness of the city.
I see the moon
and the moon sometimes
turns bad upon you.

## VII

Five years dead
Five years of reanimation
but now
I know not
Am I alive
Or dragging my life

## *Story of the Camel*

### I

Yesterday I ate
All the files of torture,
All the African struggle against Apartheid
The history of abduction,
All the indigestible city of Cairo
And this morning I'm still hungry
I don't know, am I dead ?

I eat very badly these days,
As if I'm on a hunger strike.

## Fleur de grenade

### VI

Because you love me,
This for you I write
If you had stayed in Lebanon I would have said:
worry not, I'm fine.
I shall dare show you all my metamorphosis.
sometimes I lose the road and try other songs
sometimes I dance alone within me
rhyming my refusal for men.
I feel alone, alone with the image of your dance.
I dance you in movements
beaming waves
deep as the Nile
waves like fire.

## Ishtar

*To Monique Bosco*

Scream Byblos, scream
against your History
against the sacrifice of a child
against the crime passed unpunished.
The cedars of your mountains shall rise and rise
forcing lightning into Soleimans temple.
And may the fire consume the lips of Ezechiel.
Who burned my eternal life.
Against all burning winds flew Artemis
against the wild pig that kill Adonis.

Against the winged lion that faced Astarte
against the sacred whore.
Towards the red water of Ishtar's hell
and all that carved the memory of there lost ones.
May vengeance move all that have been hurt.
May vengeance guide all from the dead.
And may the earth tremble with terror, to release you . . .
. . . Byblos
You and all your thorny kings that once ruled
from green to desert.
The Pheonix is dying
holding the redness of your blood shells on its wings
bursting your waters with fire.


## Between the Rivers

That is my Exile
That which was not only forced by war
But which stems out of our entangled roots
Roots that go so deep touching the sense of life inside us.
For why search for origins
And never have answers
For why make differences
When really nothing is different
Yet still we search for the great difference
Between cultures
Between instinct and customs
Between loving till death
or dying till love
to be able to live with others or
not be able to live at all.
My ethics try to make peace
With all cultures and cults that are in me
in me or outside

it's all the same
I admit
I don't know
The more I write
The less I know.

*Translated from the French by Shérif Ltaif*

# YAMINA MOUHOUB

## THE MOMENT MATTERS NOT

### *The Prisoner*

white in daylight
black at night

the grinding fear
the upheld breath

white in daylight
black at night

Algiers
the city opened
to the scavengers
to the malicious
to the stray dogs
to the crawling monsters

white in daylight
black at night

Algiers the prisoner

# *Shceherazade*

Scheherazade, my sister,
marathon – storyteller
tell us
over and over again
how
timesaver in torment
you keep track of the days
tell the night
how
Oracle of the Orient
at each new dawn
at each new breath
your lips span out
your story, your life.

Scheherazade
forever favorite
awaiting her sentence
tell your sisters
one thousand times
and once more
how
in a sesame secret
in one everlasting night
you trapped
in your story's web
of unheard wonders,
from Sindbad the Sailor
to Aladdin the Genie,
the mortal desire
of your executioner Sultan.

## Trivial Is the Time

trivial is the time
the place, the sigh

trivial is the unwanted word
the persistence of silence

trivial is the skin-deep emotion
the beating pulse

trivial is the fugitive sun
in frosty mornings

trivial is the time
the place, the souvenir picture

when all is gone
of what was once.

## Peace

Did we have to die
every day
before we could celebrate peace?

Did we have to lose it
forever
before we could appreciate it?

Outer misfortune!
Did we have to surrender
our lives
to desperation's will?

# *Winter*

Winter O Winter
whatever happened
to the color green
to the birds' twittering
death-scented winter
squalid winter
teeth-chattering
light-shutting winter.

over-white
immaculate winter
I color you saffron yellow
and horizon blue.

harassing and persecuting
piercing winter
chilling my blood.

I stand against you, winter
my body
wielding blazes
of living images
born in other climates.

long-distance winter
I go through you
as I would go through
a desert

at the pace of a camel-driver
familiar with quicksands
loaded with supplies
his head full

of the same mirage
of an oasis, somewhere
in the immensity
of his desire.

## To Write

To write in pen and ink
unexpectedly
at point-blank
the love of words
drifting
swaying
like seaweed
on the water surface
to be hauled up on the white
smooth beach

To write as
a gift of life
the foremost cry
all alone in darkness
evening silence
with the help of nobody

To write, to say
the phosphorescence
of immediate desire
caught
in raptured eyes
in the moist quivering
of the hand
the emotion which alters
voice sound

To write in the canvas net
myriads of scripts
fervent scribe
imprint your thread your signature
your stamp your hieroglyph
your graffiti
on the rock of time

To write.

## The Cry

The cry of a surviving
fleeing animal
and the stone-cold
silence
my tongue
a vestige
of human oblivion
wavers, falters
stumbles,
tries wildly
all over again
between outcry
and voicelessness.

## Ariadne's Thread

it was a long road
which brought me to you

a Corinthian labyrinth
without Ariadne's thread

a journey through hell
without the color of hope

a crossing of the desert
burning deep in my soul

a sinister Milky Way
a dead-end without a name

and then light coming
through the grey of the fog

you.

## Sorrow

when sorrow
takes hold
of reason

when reason
sinks
amid questions

I would rather be a stone
conversing with the wind

I would rather be a rock
as well as the ocean's sister

the lost pebble
in a child's hand.

# Gazelle

if by any chance gazelle
you look beyond
that sandy horizon
remember gazelle
that the faith hunter
is constantly on the lookout
for you to blunder

I fear for you gazelle
fatal are
the adverse times
when beauty is an offense
and crime
a blessing.

*Translated from the French by Assia Mouhoub-Sassi*

# RUBA NADDA

## DAUGHTER OF PALESTINE

## *The Wind Blows Towards Me Particularly*

I step into the art gallery and leave the July air behind. It's very hot. We're having one of those humid days where they warn everyone not to go out but everyone does anyway. I like hot days. The winters in Canada make me not mind the blistering heat that has come to visit the city. Water running down my face is almost comforting to me.

The July air hangs everywhere, I can touch it, see it dancing in the four o'clock heat. The air conditioning is broken, I listen to the complaints of the people around me. My hand wipes the sweat off my face. People look at me.

There are people everywhere. There is supposed to be a grand exhibition going on. I don't know any of the painters, I just love to look at the work, that's all. It's the renaissance paintings that draw my attention. The women with the long, long hair that flows to their knees and the pale white faces. I stand and stare at these paintings for what seems like hours. I make up stories behind them. The grand clock chimes again, and I look at it. It's only been an hour.

I take off my silk black gloves and tuck them into my straw bag. My husband won't be home until six. I'm glad too because it gives me an hour. No one's home. I always take advantage of this. I hate being watched and asked all the time where I'm going and why I should have someone accompanying me. I'm twenty three, I'm old enough to take care of myself. But my family, they all think it's dangerous to walk alone.

I glance at my watch with the leather wristband. The heat gets to me for a quick second. It passes and I decide to sit down.

There's a cafe in the middle of this art gallery. I am taken with the architecture. Taken with the high ceilings and intricate carvings on the walls. I buy a cold drink and take a seat by the fountain.

I want to raise my veil. No one important is here to see me do it. People who come and go, look at me. And sometimes I wish I were invisible.

The veil hides my face. I feel it grow heavy from the heat. My hand wanders up to touch it and I'm relieved to find that it's not drenched in sweat.

Two young girls stop to look at me. They say something about how beautiful I am. They think I can't speak English. They talk slowly to me, I tell them I can speak. I was born here after all. I have a B.A. from U of T. They want to take a picture of me. I shake my head. They walk away, still talking about me.

But I'm happy. I feel good. I like being alone. I look at my watch again and see I have fifty minutes. It usually takes him fifteen minutes on the subway and maybe another ten minutes for walking. I'll take a taxi and beat him there. His mother is visiting her daughter who is married and living in some suburb, I forget the name. I don't really like the daughter. She's too religious for my taste. She's pregnant and she's only been married for one month. In my religion, my culture, you have to have a child as soon as you get married. Or people will talk. Say shitty things about you. Then, after the first child, you can go on the pill.

I can't have children. I'm happy about that too.

I sip my drink. I don't let go of it. I like the cold feeling on my warm hand. There are voices all around me. Next time I come, I want to bring paper and write. Conversations everywhere, I don't know which one to listen to. I start fanning myself with the program.

They are playing classical music. Vivaldi. If I close my eyes, I'm in a different world.

I look out the window and watch the sun disappear. It's quite a beautiful sight. The sky turns many colors. I try to memorize the image so that when I get back home, I can write it down.

A young couple sit close to me. The girl stares and doesn't take her eyes off of me. I look away. She's not that great looking. One of those typical blonds with the mousy hair. My black hair is freshly washed but nobody knows that.

Her boyfriend, I know it's her boyfriend by the way they touch and speak to each other, is very good looking. His long hair is pushed back because of the sweat and heat but his pale face with the beads of sweat make me look at him.

He looks back at me. I run my fingers along the silver edge of the table, it makes me shiver. He doesn't look at me, he looks at my hand. Then at me. He smiles and looks away.

A new piece comes on. I want them to turn it up higher. I want the music to go through me.

A group of elderly women pass by me, gossiping about

this and that. I am reminded to call my mother tonight. I turn to my right. I am taken by these two girls. One of them is crying very hard. I feel sorry for her. It's the two girls who wanted to take my picture. She was fine when she asked me and I'm curious as to why this sudden mood change has happened. She's saying how she's in a lot of trouble. Something about losing a job and failing an exam.

"I wonder if she's hot."

I turn and look at the couple. I know she's talking about me. I wasn't born in the water, you know.

Her boyfriend was also looking at the two girls.

I take out a Kleenex from my purse. I'm even tempted to put some lipstick on, but I decide not to.

I wonder what exam she failed. I decide to remember that detail too.

"Why does she wear all of that?"


I know the plain girl is looking at me, I don't give her the satisfaction of looking back.

I wipe my face with my Kleenex. I put it on the table.

Outside, it's suddenly become very windy. I knew this heat would be washed away. The wind blows towards me particularly. The skies have become grey and drops of rain hit the hot, sizzling pavement. I hear the thunder, hear the lightening.

I glance at my watch.

"I wonder what she looks like." she says.

It seems she's confused. I guess she has the stereotype that because I'm wearing this veil, I have to have brown skin and black colored eyes.

Well I don't.

I'm white. As white as milk, as white as the light from my desk lamp when I'm writing late at night. And my eyes are blue. Very bright like the color of rain. I'm not a stereotype.

"People like that piss me off. She wears the veil so other men won't feel attracted to her. She's in Canada now. Who would be attracted to her here?"

"Keep your voice down."

I look at her now. She thinks that because she's whispering, I won't hear her. People like that really kill me.

I look at my watch. I should get going soon or else get stuck in the thunderstorm. They said it was coming on the radio but I didn't believe them.

I try to listen to the couple's conversation now.

"I can't make it tomorrow."

"But you promised –"

"I know and I feel bad."


" I can't believe you," she says. "I can't go alone."

"Why not?"

She is flustered. "I don't know. Because."

"I promise, I'll make it up to you."

"Why did you promise me then, if you knew you were going to back out?"

"I didn't know I'd be this behind."

"You're just making excuses. You don't want to go."

"Come on," he says, holding her – touching her arm. "My paper is due in a couple of days. This is important."

"Well, why haven't you started it yet?"

"I've been thinking about it."

"I didn't think I'd be playing second fiddle to words."

"You sound stupid."

I can see he said the wrong thing. She's really getting mad.

"It wasn't like this when we met a year ago."

I want to interrupt and tell her that people change with time. And change shouldn't be taken as a negative thing.

"I guess it wasn't."

I don't know who to concentrate on. At the beginning, they were all paying attention to me. Now it seemed they were so in deep with their problems, it reversed, it's me who's watching them. I'm the watcher. I like that.

The rain starts to fall, very hard. It darkens outside and the clouds move quickly. The two girls and the couple, they don't even look outside. The rain hits the windows and everyone outside runs to safety. I glance at my watch. I'm going to be late if I don't leave now.

I pick up my Kleenex again to wipe my face.

I look at the couple. Silence. I wonder if this is the end for them.

"Well now what?"

"I don't know," he says.

She looks at him for a long time before saying anything. The girl who was crying is still crying, twice as hard now. She's got another 'big' problem that her friend is trying to get out of her. I wonder what it is. I look at them closely and realize they aren't friends but sisters. They're wearing khaki shorts and white blouses. The crying girl is clutching her black handbag. She's beautiful. Even when she's desperate. The other girl, her hair is shorter, she seems to be more aggressive, stronger.

I look back at the couple. The lightening stops time and them gallery is lit and all of our faces are a pale blue. The thunder sings as loudly as she can.

I catch some words from the couple and look at them again.

" . . . hasn't been right between us. And it's not like we haven't tried."

She looks at him. She can't believe he just said those words.

"You don't know the meaning of anything."

I wonder what the meaning of anything is.

"I think I do Leanna. The world doesn't revolve around you."

No, it revolves around me. I almost laugh out loud, but I don't.

"I guess it doesn't." Her voice is very bitter. "I guess we're not going to take that long walk we've been talking about."

"I guess not."


"So this is it."

He doesn't answer her. He just looks away. To me. Then looks back at her.

"I hope your paper goes well."

They don't know I watch them. They have no idea.

"Thanks."

I wonder how they can be so formal with one another when they've done so much, when so much has happened between them.

The girl, Leanna, bends down to pick up her bag. She glances at me. I wipe the beads of sweat from my face with my Kleenex again. She walks away without saying goodbye. My hands start shaking. I don't know why. I can't make them stop.

"Oh God, oh God, oh God." The girl who is crying has her face hidden in her hands.

The guy looks at me. I look at him too, I don't look away. My hands still shake. I don't want him to talk to me.

He looks at the painting close to me. I wipe the sweat from my face.

"Hello."

I look at him. He's talking to me. I can't talk to him. It's not a good thing if he hears my voice.

"Are you waiting for someone?"

I look around. Why don't I just get up and leave?

"Can you speak English?"

I don't say anything.

"Do you need any help?"

"I can't talk to you," my voice is low and nice.

He goes to say something but doesn't. He gives me a strange look. He gets up and studies the painting around the cafe. Most of the people have left. All I can hear is the pretty girl crying, her muffled sobs make my insides ache. I want to tell her that everything will be okay, no matter how awful everything seems now.

"Amazing paintings." He looks at me for a second before looking at the paintings.

"They're frighteningly realistic."

I look at them.

"Yes."

He stops and looks at me. I know he's being careful. I wonder what his hair feels like. Must feel nice, soft. He pushes it out of his eyes. I really want to touch him. I have this urge to. Maybe that's why my hands are shaking and my breathing is steady. His white shirt and blue jeans make him look very thin. The sleeves are rolled up.

He looks at the painting that's near the exit.

"I wonder – I wonder about that painting. Beautiful, isn't it?"

I look at it.

"Yes."

He looks at me.

I glance at my watch. Now, he will know I have gone somewhere. He'll enter the house, call my name and I won't be there to respond to his endless wishes. I won't be there to make him his tea, or listen carefully to the stories he tells me of his job. I won't be there to prepare him dinner and then wash the dishes while he relaxes on the sofa. I won't be there to serve him his cold drink later on in the evening and to sit by him and watch television. I won't even be there when his mother comes home and tells him how proud she is of her daughter. How beautiful the child is. How she wishes – how she just wishes, I would be cured. I'm not going to be there when they tell me when my next doctor's visit will be. I won't be there when they tell their stories – their disgust at how this western culture is going straight to hell. Or listen to his shock about how he was on the subway and this young couple were kissing. Hear him say to me that is one of the reasons why he forbids me to ride the subway alone. Why I must never go out alone. I won't even be there when late at night, he'll take a long hot bath and expect his weekly appetite to be fulfilled. I just won't be there. And I smile to the idea, to the picture I've created. Because I'm tired of him.

The rain hits and hits and I want it to never stop. I wonder how much money I've got in my wallet.

"What do you wonder?" I ask him.

He looks at me, confused.

I point and say, "At the painting."

He shrugs. "It's so desolate, yet – yet . . . "

"Peaceful"

"Peaceful?"

"Yeah."

"Are you an artist?" I ask him.

"No," and he laughs. "No, I'm not."

He looks at me.

"What do you do?" I ask him.

There's the lightening again. And I forget his eyes are blue.

"I don't know. I don't know."


I get up. He stares at my hands. They probably intrigue him. They are very white. I go to pick up my bag but spill my drink instead. I'm embarrassed. It runs across the table and starts dripping over the side. I watch it. He doesn't know what to say. He moves closer to me. The two girls are quiet. She's stopped crying. She's trying to convince herself that everything will be okay. She keeps saying it over and over again. The other girl is patting her shoulder. He goes to move closer.

I move and he stops.

I raise my veil. My face breathes. He turns away.

My hand wavers in the air, remains like that for a second. He doesn't move away. My hand slumps down and I feel the cold drink I spilt on my fingers.

"I have to go." But I don't go anywhere.

"Stay for a while." He comes forward. I don't turn away. I don't want to.

"Go back to your precious Canadian life."

The wind howls. It makes an eerie sound as it hits itself against the windows.

I touch the side of his face. I don't think. I concentrate on the music. I run my fingers over his eyes, his forehead. I touch his hair. He moves closer to me. He bends down. I put my hand behind his neck and bring him towards me. I kiss him.

Doors open and the calling wind hits me like the wind from an approaching subway train coming out of a tunnel. And I ignore it.

Because I think God left the art gallery for sure.

## Daughter of Palestine

I lost my home.

One day, I woke up with the tv still on and I realized I lost my home. My daughters do not understand me. They always ask me, why do you want fancy couches, fancy home?

They do not understand, I am daughter of Palestine. I never had a home. Two sisters and one brother died in the war of '67.

They died because their ears blew from the guns over top. My mamma was sitting under the olive tree, their green little eyes just wouldn't close, staring up at the heavens like that. And she knew they were dead.

My mamma was a Syrian, she was given as a gift to her husband.

My mamma never had a home either.

My mamma always had something to prove. Three of

her kids died in her arms. I see her in my dreams. Her hands calling to me. But when I go to her, she tells me I am not ready yet. I need a home first.

My daughters, they dress in their jeans and talk to me in fancy English. They talk too fast, I don't understand. They live fancy life. I tell my eldest, you are daughter of Syria. She says no.

No.

I am not Arabic. I am French.

She was born in Montreal. Maybe tomorrow she will understand. Her blood is Arab. Her hair coarse, her eyebrows thick. She is daughter of Syria.

They sit laughing at me on the stupid tattered couch. We have safety pins holding it together. They don't know I shake with anger inside. My curses, my tears they do not hear. I muffle with a towel in the bathroom.

Their father holds back the money from me.

I have no home. They took it from me when I was three. I remember. My babba picking up my brother and running out of the flaming house. It was my mamma who saved me. We never had a home. Even when we lived in Syria, we were foreigners.

The wind is shifting. They think I am stupid. I don't care.

I just want a home.

I am a good person, done some bad things. But that's okay.

I deserve a home.

Home where no one will ask me to leave from.

Home where I can put gold everywhere. Laugh. Laugh all you want.

I am daughter of Palestine.

You pretty girl, I taught you how to speak.

You are daughter of Syria.
I made mistake.
I made mistake.
I am fifty three and I still have no home.
Mistake. Mistake.

# BIO-BIBLIOGRAPHIES

Anne-Marie Alonzo: Poet, translator, playwright, literary critic, Anne-Marie Alonzo was born in Alexandria, Egypt, on December 13, 1951. She came to Québec in 1963. In July, 1966, she was victim of a car accident which left her quadriplegic. Her work bears the indelible mark of this tragedy. Anne-Marie Alonzo is the most prolific of the writers portrayed here. She has authored twenty books, among which *Bleu de mine* which won her the prestigious Émile Nelligan Award for poetry in 1985. That same year, she founded, along with Alain Laframboise, a literary journal, *Trois*, and a publishing house bearing the same name. In 1992, Alonzo received Le Grand Prix d'Excellence Artisitque de Laval. In 1997, she received the Order Of Canada Award. She holds a PH.D. in literature from the Université de Montréal. The above excerpt is from *Lead Blues*, pp. 11-23.

*Geste*, Paris, Éditions des femmes, 1979. Poetic fragments.

*Veille*, Paris, Éditions des Femmes, 1982. Poetic fragments

*Blanc de thé*. Montréal, Les Zéditions élastiques, 1983. Object-book.

*Droite et de profil*, Montréal, Lèvres urbaines 7, 1984. Poetic fragments.

*Une lettre rouge, orange et ocre*, Montréal, Éditions de la pleine lune, 1984. Dramatic text.

*Der ungeschriebene brief, Bremen,* FRG, Xenia, 1991. Translation by Traude Bührmann of *Une lettre rouge, orange et ocre*

*Bleus de mine*, Ville St-Laurent, Éditions du Noroît, 1985. Poetry.

*Lead Blues*, translated with a preface by W. Donoghue. Montréal, Guernica, 1990. Fiction.

*French Conversation*, Laval, Éditions Trois, 1986. Book of Texts and pictures. In collaboration with Alain Laframboise.

*Nous en reparlerons sans doute*, Laval, Éditions Trois, 1986. In collaboration with Denise Desautels and Raymonde April. Book of texts and photographs.

*Écoute Sultane*. Montréal, Éditions de l'Hexagone, 1987. Fiction.

*Seul le désir*, Montréal, NBJ éditeur, 1987. Poetic fragments.

*Le Livre des ruptures*, Montréal, Éditions de l'Hexagone, 1988. Poetry.

*Bleu de mine,* Montréal, Guernica, 1990. Translation by W. Donoghue of *Lead Blues*.

*L'Immobile* , Montréal, L'Hexagone , 1990. Letters.

*Galia qu'elle nommait Amour*, Montréal, Éditions Trois, 1992. Tale.

*Margie Gilli*s, *La danse des marches*, Montréal, Éditions du Noroît, 1993.
   Poetic fragments.
*Tout au loin la lumière*, Montréal, Éditions du Noroît, 1994. Poetry.
*Lettres à Cassandre*, Laval, Éditions Trois, 1994 In collaboration with Denise
   Desautels. Poetry.

Andrée Dahan: Born in Cairo, Egypt. She came to Québec in 1968.
She received a master's degree from the Université de Montréal in
1975 and soon after, she began publishing in local magazines. She
taught language and literature in Egypt, France, Morocco and Québec;
she was a lecturer at the Université du Québec between 1986 and
1993. She is currently working on her third novel. The above excerpt
is from her 1985 novel, *Le Printemps peut attendre*, pp. 21-36.

*Le Printemps peut attendre*, Montréal, Quinze, 1985. Novel.
*L'Exil aux portes du paradis*, Montréal, Québec-Amérique, 1993. Novel.

Abla Farhoud: Born in Lebanon, Abla Farhoud went to Québec in
1951. She embarked on an acting career at the age of seventeen,
appearing on Canadian and Lebanese television. She studied theatre at
the Université de Paris VIII and received an MA in Theatre Arts with a
specialization in play writing from the Université du Québec à Montréal. Abla Farhoud is internationally recognized as an emerging voice
in contemporary Francophone literature. She has written, to date,
eight plays which have been performed in Canada, France, Belgium,
Lebanon, and the United States. Her works have been published in
both French and English. In 1993, she was honored with the prix
Arletty de l'Universalité de la langue française (Arletty Universality of
the French Language Award) and the prix Théatre et Liberté de la
Société des Auteurs Dramatiques de France (Theatre and Liberty
Award of the French Society of Authors and Composers). She has also
written short stories, radio scripts and monologues. Her first novel, *Le
bonheur a la queue glissante* (Montréal: L'Hexagone 1998), has been
nominated for the Prix France/Québec. Abla Farhoud is currently
living in Montreal and working on a second novel, *Splendide solitude*.
The above excerpts are from her novel, *Le Bonheur a la queue glissante,* pp. 9-18, pp. 37-46, pp. 147-153, respectively.

*Splendide solitude,* in Progess. Novel.

*Les Filles du 5-10-15,* Editions Lansman, Carnière, Belgium, 1995. Play.
*The Girls from the Five and Ten,* in *Plays By Women; An International Anthology,* New York, Ubu Repertory Theatre Publications, 1988
*Quand le vautour danse,* Editions Lansman, Carnière, Belgium, 1997. Play.
*Le Bonheur a la queue glissante.* Montréal, L'Hexagone, 1998. Novel
*Jeux de patience.* Montréal, Vlb éditeur, 1997. Play.
*Game of Patience.* Translation by Jill McDougall of *Jeux de patience.,* in *Plays By Women; II, An International Anthology,* New York, Ubu Repertory Theatre, Publications, 1994.
*Quand j'étais grande,* in *Le Bruit des autres,* Montréal, Solignac, 1994.
*When I was Grown Up,* in *Women & Performance* 5:1 New York, 1989.

Yolande Geadah: Born in Egypt. She has been living in Montréal since 1967. She is a Consultant in International Development. She has been working for the last twenty years for the Canadian ONG (non governmental organisations). She has completed course-work towards a PH.D. at the Université du Québec à Montréal. She has published many articles on questions related to women in developing countries. Yolande Geadah's *Femmes voilées* (1996) was one of the finalists for the Governor General Award (Best Essay). The above excerpt is from her book, *Femmes voilées, Intégrismes démasqués,* pp. 203-221

*Femmes voilées, Intégrismes démasqués,* Montréal, VLB, 1996. Essay.
Co-author of *Un autre genre de développement* (English title:*Two Halves make a Whole; Balancing Gender Relations in Development*) Conseil canadien de coopération internationale, Association québécoise des organismes de coopération internationale, Ottawa, Montréal, 1991. Case-Studies.
*L'Influence de l'Islam sur les femmes dans les projets de développement; trois études portant sur les cas de l'Egypte, du Soudan et du Niger,* Ottawa, Agence canadienne de développement international, 1989, 1990, 1992. Case-Studies.

Nadia Ghalem: Born in Algeria. She came to Montreal in 1965. She worked for thirty years as a journalist and a writer for Radio-Canada and TV Ontario. She collaborated in numerous French reviews in Quebec, Italy and Louisiana. She was a finalist for numerous literary prizes. In 1993, her novel, *La Rose des sable,* received the CREDIF Prize (Paris). Nadia Ghalem is very active as member of the Board of Directors of many organisations, such as SARDEC (Société des auteurs recherchistes et documentalistes) and Conseil de Presse du Québec. She has given numerous poetry recitals. In 1995, she obtained a

Master's degree in Communication from the Université du Québec à Montréal. Nadia Ghalem's novel, *La Villa désir* (1988) was a finalist for the 1987 Grand Prix Littéraire Guérin. The above excerpt is from her collection of short stories, *La Nuit bleue*, pp. 17-27.

*L'Oiseau de fer,* Sherbroooke, Naaman, 1980. Short stories.
*Les Jardins de cristal* , Québec, Hurtubise 1981. Novel.
*L'Exil*, édition tirage limité par Les Compagnons du lion d'or, Dépôt légal, Bibliothèque Nationale du Québec, 1980. Poetry.
*La Villa désir*, Montréal, Guérin littérature, 1988. Novel.
*La Nuit bleue*, Montréal, VLB éditeur, 1991. Short Stories.
*La Rose des sables*, Québec, Hurtubise, 1993. Children's story.
*Le Huard et le Héron*. Montréal: Les Editions du Trécarré, 1995. Youth story.

Mona Latif Ghattas: Poet, playwright, novelist and film director, Mona Latif Ghattas was born in Egypt and has been living in Montreal since 1966. She has participated in a number of international conferences and has given many poetry recitals in several countries, notably in Belgium, France, Egypt and Canada. Her books are often listed in the curriculum of universities such as Institut Simone de Beauvoir (Concordia University). The above excerpt is from her novel, *Le Double conte de l'exil*, pp. 9-17.

*Les Chants du Karawane,* Le Caire, Elias Publishing House, 1985. Poetic moments.
*Quarante voiles pour un exil,* Montréal, Éditions Trois, 1986. Poetic fragments.
*Le Double conte de l'exil*. Montréal: Boréal, 1990. Novel.
*Les Voix du jour et de la nuit*. Montréal: Boréal, 1988. Novel.
*Nicolas, le fils du Nil*. Cairo: Elias Publishing House, 1985. Poetic novel.
*Ma chambre belge*, Belgium, L'Arbre à paroles, 1991. Poem.
*La Triste beauté du monde*, Montréal, Éditions du Noroît, 1993. Poetry.
*Les Lunes de miel*, Montréal, Leméac, 1996. Narratives.

Nadine Ltaif: Of Lebanese descent, Nadine Ltaif, a well-published poet, was born in Cairo in 1961. She studied in Lebanon. She came to Montreal in 1980 and received a master's degree in French Studies from the Université de Montréal. She is on the editorial board of the Canadian bilingual review, *Tessera*. The above excerpts are from *Les Métamorphoses d'Ishtar*, pp. 9, 10, 12, 7, 11, 43, and 33, respectively, and *Entre les fleuves*, pp. 28.

*Les Métamorphoses d'Ishtar,* Montréal, Guernica, 1987.
*Entre les fleuves,* Montréal, Guernica, 1991.
*Élégies du Levant,* Éditions du Noroît, Saint Laurent, 1995.
*Le livre des dunes,* Éditions du Noroît, Saint Laurent, 1999.

Yamina Mouhoub: A Canadian citizen, Yamina Mouhoub was born in 1939 in Medjana, Algeria. She holds a Bachelor degree (1994) in French Studies from the Université de Montréal. She is a prolific writer who has devoted many years working in the field of pre-school and elementary school pedagogy. She has published in a number of literary magazines such as *L'Iris Espace* (Paris), *Envol* (Ottawa), *Inédit nouveau* (La Huppe, Belgium) and she belongs to several literary associations in Quebec, such as Société Littéraire de Laval and Union des Auteurs et Artistes Africains au Canada. The above excerpt is from her book of poetry, *Qu'Importe le moment,* pp. 9, 17, 31, 34, 35, 49, 54, 61, 63, 73.

*Qu'importe le moment,* Laval, Teichtner, 1999. Poetry.
"Jours de cendre," in *Les poètes du dimanche,* Volume IV, Andrésy, France, 1998, page 98.
"Timimoun," in *Les poètes du dimanche,* Volume IV, Andrésy, France, 1998, pp. 99-100.
"Et pourtant elle tourne" in *Les poètes du dimanche,* Volume V, Andrésy, France, 1999, pp. 103-104.

Ruba Nadda: Ruba Nadda is an Arab-Canadian writer/filmmaker, living in Toronto. She was born in Montréal. Her parents came to Canada in the seventies from Damascus, Syria, where Rubba herself lived for three years on several occasions. Many of her short stories have been published internationally, in journals such as *Riversedge Journal, Blood & Aphorisms, White Wall Review, Wascana Review,* etc. She has made 12 short films, to mention, "Blue Turning Grey Over You" (1999), "Black September" (1999), "I would suffer cold hands for you" (1999), "Laila (1999). They all deal with Arabs and have been shown in film festivals over 65 times in five countries: Rotterdam Film Festival, Sweden, Vienna, Germany and Toronto. She has just finished her first feature film, *I Always Come to You.* The above excerpt is from *Daughter of Palestine .*

*Daughter of Palestine.* Toronto, Sister Vision Press. In Press. Short Stories
*Promised Land.* Toronto, Sister Vision Press. In Press. Short stories.

Farida Elizabeth Dahab was born in London, England, and grew up in Cairo, Egypt, in a francophone family. A trilingual Canadian Citizen, she received a B.A. in Psychology from McGill University and a Master's of Education in Educational Psychology from the University of Alberta. She obtained her doctorate in Comparative Literature from the Université de Paris IV-Sorbonne (France). She has held faculty positions in French/francophone Literatures in Arizona, California, and Missouri. She is currently a member of the Department of Comparative World Literature and Classics at California State University, Long Beach. She has published a number of articles and given conference papers on literatures of lesser diffusion, especially on Arabic-Canadian literature.